Good Cop

GOOD COP

JIM ALEXANDER

Planet Jimbot

Glasgow

For Dad

1.

Word Up

I was in bed. Well, the majority of me was. My right leg was sticking out from under the duvet. The rogue foot flopped down to the floor; toes scrunched against the coarseness of the carpet. It was like my body occupied two very different states. On the one hand there was the warmth of my bed, an oasis, insulating me from the world around me. And then there was my rebellious foot pressing down against a perfunctory sterile bedroom carpet, which wasn't welcoming—which wasn't designed to be welcoming. Instead, it was a portal to something rough and inhospitable.

It was 5.45 in the morning, but try telling my brain that. It was boiling like an expectant kettle, sloshing, careering from one unfinished sentence to another. No matter the cul-de-sac my brain was intent on taking me, I eventually deferred to my foot and, following its lead, rolled out of bed. You could say it was all downhill from there. To underline the point, I tumbled downstairs, and even though I had more than enough time to prepare something more substantial, I had a packet of salt and vinegar crisps for breakfast.

I was aware of how tawdry my action was—lazy, worthless, tatty—but at no point did I consider this a good reason to stop. With every crunch of every crisp my irritation levels increased, but I kept on crunching regardless. My senses, those senses that mattered most in the morning, happy to greedily absorb the acidic salty taste. Almost absent-mindedly, the tip of my tongue chased some food residue around the inside of my mouth. It embraced globules of masticated mush and saliva. For some reason, maybe no reason, the image of dung beetles from some nature TV documentary nudged into my brain, pushing balls of—well, the clue was in the name. I put down the crisps, no longer having the enthusiasm to tip out and finish the fragments which lay at the bottom of the packet. I'd only been up twenty minutes and I was already wishing this miserable day was over.

'Come on, JS,' I said to myself because, let's face it, there was no one else around to say it, 'get that bahookie of yours in the shower.'

I got dressed and went to work. Or specifically, wherever work would take me.

I was called out to an Airbnb in Clarkston. The scene of the crime. To be fair, if a crime hadn't been committed, I'd have had no reason to be there.

On arrival, I found PC McIntyre was already in

attendance. I'd no sooner walked through the front door when he had a quiet word in my ear. 'Ma'am...' he began.

I listened intently, even though I was conscious of the stubble around PC McIntyre's chin now perilously close to the side of my face. And I tried not to be too judgemental. I tried, in my mind, not to question what had led him to decide not to shave that morning. It was my mind, after all, and it should do what it was told. At least his breath seemed fine. There was nothing to suggest he'd had whisky with his cornflakes.

Quiet word concluded, I left PC McIntyre to it and strode into the kitchen area. It was there that I found a man and woman, two holidaymakers hailing from Dorset. They were both having a cup of tea. The man had thinning hair which belied his age, which I was to discover was in the early thirties. The woman's hair was tied in a perfect bow. I could not fault it. You saw the prettiest things at a crime scene.

The couple seemed to be in good spirits which, unlike the hair, caught me off guard considering the circumstances. They looked up and stared at me and waited patiently for me to speak. I swallowed and blinked and delayed talking until the constituent parts which made up my composure slid into place. It wasn't a big thing, but all the same, I waited for the click.

'Hi,' I said. 'I am Detective Sergeant Spencer. And you are...' I half-glanced at my notes. 'Adam Burrows and Susan Earnshaw.' I got the tiniest of nods from the former.

The latter broke into a broad smile, which appeared to me to be, I guess, genuine.

I said, 'How are you?'

'All right.'

'Can't complain.'

This wasn't the reaction you'd expect from victims of crime. Especially victims of *recent* crime. For a second, I thought I'd taken a wrong turn and arrived at the wrong address. But this would have meant PC McIntyre having arrived on his own speed at the wrong address as well. The *same* wrong address, incidentally.

'The facts, as I understand them: you were both tied up and threatened with an axe by an unknown assailant,' I said. 'Your attacker fled when the police were called out by a suspicious neighbour who had earlier challenged your assailant on why he was carrying an axe. He wasn't convinced by the response that he was a man from the council, who was also a professional tree surgeon, assigned with the task of cutting down a silver birch.'

Another nod and another smile, but nothing that would indicate panic from Adam Burrows and Susan Earnshaw, or even mild alarm.

Mr Burrows massaged one of his wrists. His expression was serene, quietly celebratory. It was PC McIntyre, first to arrive on the scene, who had untied them, and I was reminded of the PC's previously hushed words which greeted me when I walked through the front door. PC McIntyre had informed me that Burrows and Earnshaw had gone on to ask if they could keep the pieces of rope used to tie their wrists together. Apparently they viewed the rope as some kind of holiday memento.

'Isn't that part of the experience?' Mr Burrows asked.

'Come again?' I asked.

'Part of the package,' Ms Earnshaw said. 'What you get when you take out an Airbnb?'

'In Scotland,' Mr Burrows added helpfully. Or at least that was his intention.

I said, 'You mean, getting tied up by a stranger pretending he was a man from the council wielding a big axe?' I'd been on the verge of prefixing the word axe with a choice swear word but stopped myself at the last second. I didn't swear. It used to be no swearing before noon, I remember, but I'd moved on since then. 'You think that's all part of the holiday Airbnb experience?'

'In Scotland?' I added hastily, not wanting to leave anything out.

'Ah-hah. Ah-hum.' In front of me, they both took on the form of nodding cats.

It wasn't long after that I got a call informing me that their attacker had been apprehended. The individual in question was a debt collector called Gary Ferguson. Fergie to his mates, which relied on the fact that he actually had any, was the unscrupulous kind of debt collector, the criminal kind. As it turned out, it was Fergie who had turned up at the wrong address. The attempt to terrorise Burrows and Earnshaw in the hope of extorting money was, in fact, a case of mistaken identity. I relayed this information to the, if not alleged, then certainly sceptical victims.

'When we get back home to Dorset, we're going to recommend the experience to all our friends,' was the response.

Statement taken, I drove back to the office to write up my report. I was at my calmest, most composed, while in transit. I could shut off a certain part of my brain. The noisy part. The part that yammered away at me and made me question what I was doing. *What was the point of my job? Did I do any good by it? What could I hope to achieve with it?* Where trying to keep my head down and get things done was concerned, this part of my brain wasn't particularly helpful.

As I drove on the Carmunnock Bypass, I freed up my mind. Well, not quite. I was thinking of the actor Patrick Stewart, who was in his eighties but was known to play characters even older than that. Jean-Luc Picard. Charles Xavier. I had developed a fascination with older bald men over the years. I've no idea where this came from, but it was something to occupy me as I waited patiently for Hugh Jackman to lose all his hair.

Flashes of Patrick Stewart gave way with a shunt to trying to remember the last time I'd had a bath. Too many showers crammed into too little a life, I reflected, as I took a left turn towards Castlemilk.

Thoughts turned to a recent incident where a man

named Tommy was hit by a car. He was still conscious when I reached the scene of the accident. He was bleeding internally, but that became apparent only later on. Directly preceding the incident, while taking his first tentative near-fatal step on the road, he claimed his attention was taken by a member of the opposite sex who was walking past on the pavement he'd just vacated. His senses dulled (I'm paraphrasing here), he didn't react to the speeding chunk of rubber and metal heading his way. Upon being asked (by me) why he wasn't paying attention to oncoming traffic, his reply went something like this:

'You should have seen the arse on it.'

Sometimes I think we're all headed for extinction. The fact that punters like Tommy do such senseless pointless things only reinforces the theory. Neanderthals, and we know what happened to them. We weren't going to last as long as *Star Trek* and see the emergence of a Captain Kirk or Picard. We weren't going to have that kind of future. We'd be as well calling off the Climate Conference to be held in the city later in the year. Referred to in some circles as the Big Show. The Big No-show more like. Our stupidity will get us first.

I kept driving. It didn't matter how much I didn't want to think about it—was prepared to think about anything else, no matter how ludicrous—the elephant was in the car. It was there sitting on the backseat with a Buddha belly and a pair of ludicrously large floppy ears. I couldn't ask how it had managed to squeeze into the back seat. I needed to pay attention. I knew where the car would take me next.

Where the car couldn't or wouldn't take me, my legs would do the rest. It was a short distance from where I parked to my intended destination, but each step seemed to take an age. Every step seemed to encompass a separate lifetime. My body trembled and I took deep breaths in a bid to shift more oxygen to my brain. If I couldn't be calm, I wouldn't be much use to anyone, myself especially. I knew where the car—and legs—would take me. How could I not know? I stared up at the flats, five storeys high, ahead of me and experienced only recognition. I had been here many times before.

Most or some of the flats were still occupied as far as I was aware. But in all the times I'd been here, I'd hardly seen a soul. It was probably too early in the day for most to consider coming out. Too light, too pre-nocturnal. Access to the building was never an issue and, once negotiated, I began to climb the stairs. As way of counterpoint to the length each step took to get here, now, as I ascended, I was only aware of every second or third stair. Snaking up each side of shifting stairs were trails of conjoined detritus, consisting of broken glass and needles. It had the same effect as hazard tape. Don't waver too close to the edge, keep on a straight path, keep on climbing, you're committed, turning back is no longer an option. I pushed past an access door hanging by its top hinges, and then I was on the roof and I couldn't climb any further.

I was outside. I was exposed. This high up there were no other buildings or impediments to break things up. There was always the wind. Untrammelled and pure. Predictable in its unpredictability. I closed my eyes and wondered if, six months ago, this was the thing that dominated his first thoughts; the wind pressing against his skin. Swirling, turning, tightening its grip on him. He was so used to being cramped in an interrogation room, out in the elements wasn't his natural element. Having been taken here against his will (at least that was the presumption) and dragged into a pure and unbroken environment. An unforgiving one.

It was time to focus on my own baby steps and I edged closer to the edge of the roof. I was close enough to peer down and, for what could have been the hundredth time, was struck by how much higher it seemed when looking down than it did looking up. Was this the point they removed the bag from over his head? It seemed as good a time as any.

And then he was falling, all five storeys, count them one by one as you go down. And then he was crashing into the sack of blood and bones safety net that was property tycoon/all-round philanthropist/feared mob boss Bryce Coleman, who was inexplicably standing on the ground below. Or maybe not that inexplicably if you believed the rumours that surrounded him. That while his henchman got their hands dirty—there wouldn't be much point in them being henchmen if they didn't—hustling the victims to the top of the roof, Coleman took a perverse pleasure on the ground looking up and watching them fall to their death. Except in this instance something went wrong. Coleman never stepped back, or to the side, or performed a handstand, or whatever he normally did to get out of the way. He didn't get clear. By all reports, certainly the important ones, he died instantly. We know the how, but as to the why, who knows? Unless we find a way to resurrect the dead, specifically one Bryce Coleman, this is destined to remain the rabid subject of endless speculation.

Who the fudge knows? Some would claim he was a monster. One of Roy Lichtenstein's most trusted lieutenants, you'd never find actual prints, but his imprint on all kinds of criminality was everywhere. And previous to this, he was untouchable, so who cares? Even so, no matter who they were, the sound of the crack of two bodies colliding must have been ear piercing. A filleted thunderclap of tissue and bone. Every time I climbed up here, I'd try to form a picture and make it clearer in my mind, only for it to seem even cloudier than the last time, and the time before that. Images that jar in my head then disperse wildly like a disturbed quarrel of sparrows. Images of twisted human fuselage.

Detective Inspector Brian Fisher. The DI. How could he have survived? Why should he have survived? Had the mystery and madness of it all infected me by default? Was this block of flats a modern standing stone, gargantuan, a beacon calling out, seeking to absorb me, disassemble me, infect me with an insanity? Was it trying to pull me inside out? Wrap me up and constrict me in its psychosis?

One thing I knew, one thing I needed to reassess in my mind, and unlike all those other times really stick to—I needed to get out more (but not come here). I really needed to get a fudging life.

2.

H Dumpty

I was in pain. I ate pain. I shat pain. I packaged pain and moved it around my body, ensuring that absolutely no part of me would be left out. Lying on part-hospital bed, part-volcanic bed of molten rock, open to no other possibility but all-consuming pain.

Searing pain. Unbearable pain.

There was a type which stood out from all others. It was the one situated around the meat of my left thigh. A dull ache that took its time, seeping through into the thigh bone. From there, it began to spread out, turning that part of me against me. It was oppressive and it extended time, the end of time. At no point did it seem like it might abate, might offer some kind of respite. It was true pain with no apparent end. Maddening pain. It made me want to sit up and rip the bone clean out of my leg. And I'd be like the song *Dem Bones*. And there would come the time when I'd try to somehow crawl out of my hospital bed. My flailing, failing hands would scramble for leverage and I'd push up and try to walk again, but my body would not work. Instead, I'd collapse in a heap. I'd be a big pile of bones.

People around me—the important people, the doctors, nurses and technicians—would no longer be there for me. They'd think, *if he can't support himself, then why should we?* Eventually they'd no longer think it. They'd now ask this question aloud and keep repeating it, volume ever increasing, until they were shouting the words. They'd have created a verbal tsunami, on the verge of forming a collective scream. It would reach a point—such a powerful thing, a beating pounding rhythm—that the sound would manifest as a physical thing. It would need to go somewhere and create an irresistible uplift, hoisting the roof right off the hospital. The heating bill would be tremendous, prohibitive as a result. It would prove too great a strain on the public purse. They'd have no choice but to shut the hospital down.

There would be nothing to keep out the icy, embittered, all-consuming damaging air. All because of a stupid children's song. *The knee bone not connected to the thigh bone.*

Broken.

My head was broken. In truth it was broken long before the fall. The fall only served to confirm what I should have known along the way. And now in my hospital bed I had plenty of time to toss such pointless thoughts—such fractured thoughts, such empty thoughts—around in my mind. I was confined to a hospital bed, limiting my worldview to the four corners of my room. There was nowhere for any of the thoughts to go, everything bouncing back at me. And it was endlessly so, like I was an unwilling participant in the world's longest ping pong game. Sometimes when the morphine found a way to sneak past the various levels, I could feel my mind loosen up, but even such a thing as this came at a cost. There was only one place I could go, and you could hardly call it an escape.

I was back there, back where I was falling through the sky. The wind nipping my earlobes back and making my eyes water. And how I longed for the tears to fall down my face, but instead they'd plummet straight down. They'd fall below me, like rain. Sometimes I wanted to holler after them—to harangue them, to go as far as threaten them—and instruct my tears to slow down, to hold their horses and wait for me to catch up. But I couldn't trust my voice. I couldn't trust what I recognised to be my voice. I knew what I wanted to say, but I couldn't rely on me having the ability to say it.

I was falling, but never to hit the bottom. My opiate release never to last long enough to allow such an eventuality to transpire. Its first throbbing apparitions would resurface, expunging the image from my brain. I was not falling. I was no longer anything. In its place, there was only the perfectly crystallised realisation that I was in agony. My body was a patchwork of bruises covering a network of broken bones. A bag of leaking scrap, of organs held together in tattered polythene.

The only part of me not screaming out in pain was the ring finger of my left hand. Or what was left of it. A lifeless stump. Chopped off by a madman who then fed it to his dog. The finger didn't appear whole, not even in my dreams. But something told me, while quiet for now, as quiet as a mouse, the stump wouldn't stay silent indefinitely.

It must have been a few years back, but I remember I was in Cumbernauld, and not for the first time. What was I doing there? It was important in my current state that I ask questions I could answer, so—

I was in pursuit of a suspect known as Slippy Ally. So called due to his uncanny ability to give the Old Bill the slip. He was running, I was running, through the streets of Cumbernauld. Despite my best efforts to make it otherwise, we were some distance apart. Too far for me to reach out and grab him and, for want of a better thing to do, wrestle him to the ground. I had the stamina and the drive and the elevated knees, but if I was gaining ground, it was ever so slowly. The situation should have been so much simpler. I should have had Slippy Ally square in my sights. He was five feet two inches in height and overweight. His belly hung round his waistline like it was a ring of Saturn. Still, he had this uncanny ability—I mentioned it before—when required, to call upon extraordinary levels of prowess. There was a rumour that he had sold his soul to the Devil in return for a touch of the supernatural about him. But in the underworld the best rumours were the ones started by the subject of the rumours themselves.

Air inflating my lungs, beads of sweat dotting the nape of my neck, I was in it for the long run. Softly, softly, catchee monkey. My feet pounded the hard concrete with so much force I could feel the vibrations travel up my hips and nestle around the base of my spine. My head dipped momentarily, an involuntary response, but I made the best of it, combining it with the will to urge myself on.

When I looked up, Slippy Ally was no longer there. Gone in less than a full blink of an eye. It was as if the ground had swallowed him whole. What was there to do but for me to lean back on my heels and come to an abrupt halt. Facing me was a front door. And not just any kind of front door. This one was ajar, ever so slightly, inviting further scrutiny.

'Remarkable,' the doctor said, having stepped into my room. He said so as he held up a picture of a blue ghost, which could have been an X-ray.

'Remarkable lungs and kidneys,' he continued, aiming to paint a more complete picture. 'Remarkable liver and intestines.'

I had been confined to a hospital bed for several weeks, and I had to confess up until this point, it had never crossed my mind to consider the state of my intestines. 'I'm here,' I said.

'You had a bad fall, Mr Fisher,' the doctor said. 'Bad as in near-fatal. The kind that probably should result in catastrophic damage at a cellular and tissue level.

The kind which should result in the type of system shutdown the body cannot fully, or even partially, recover from.'

'Mister as in Detective,' the doctor added hastily.

'I'm here. I can hear you.'

'All we can do is wait and hope, carry out blood transfusions and intravenous therapy, pat down your pillows, and make things as comfortable as possible for you. What we're looking for, strictly speaking, is a surge from within. We're in the lap of the gods. '

'I can hear you. Can you hear me?'

'Your body not only has to send up a flare...' The doctor withdrew one of his hands, leaving a single hand delegated to holding aloft the X-ray, which was hardly any hardship at all. A finger, its emancipation short-lived, subsequently despatched to scratch, languorously so, the side of his nose. 'Your body also needs to answer it. Yes, a surge is what is needed. A surge in gene and immune activity. A jump-start. Imagine something like a night in late November in Carluke, the moment when the council turns on the town's Christmas Lights.'

The doctor's digit scratching ceased, freeing his hand again, this time to hover over his left cheek. He pressed two fingers into the cheekbone and began to massage it with his fingertips, demonstrating little in the way of finesse. As they moved around, his fingers left an imprint on the skin like it was putty. His eyes narrowed in line with the increase in pressure he seemed to exert, as if searching for signs of discomfort.

I wanted to say something. I wanted to ask after his general welfare. I wanted the doctor to know that I cared. But all logic dictated that such attempts would go the way of all my previous stabs at communication and fall on deaf ears.

The doctor's hand dropped to his jaw, which he held in a pinch between thumb and index finger. Then he turned with a flurry. The back of his lab coat lifted momentarily, corresponding to his movement like it was a gentleman's cape.

'Remarkable intestines,' he said again, before making his way out.

It was then that I realised my jaw, having undergone surgery much like the rest of me, was wired up. And I wondered if my voice had indeed belonged to me, or perhaps belonged to something else. If not me, perhaps it was the blue ghost all along.

Not that any of that mattered. It might have done minutes before, but not now. Instead, I was relieved that the doctor hadn't gone on to comment on any other part of my body.

But any feeling of relief wasn't meant to last, not in my present condition, no siree, giving way to—

Cumbernauld, for the uninitiated, is a New Town which came into being in the mid-50s. It was conceived to help alleviate the demand for housing in nearby Glasgow. One of the things about a New Town, Cumbernauld included—such was the egalitarian outlook of the town planners of the time—is that the houses were designed to be all the same. The streets were all the same. The corner shops were all the same. Still, the town had a special place in the hearts of people of a certain vintage. In the '80s there were a series of promotional TV ads designed to promote the town, coining the phrase, the clarion call: 'What's it called? Cumbernauld.'

All in all, I'd had cause to visit the town seventeen times—mostly in a professional capacity. For my seventeenth time, there was just cause to push the door further open, so allowing me to enter a hall which quickly gave way to a flight of stairs. The tread of my shoe made its acquaintance with the bottom stair. My weight shifted, giving birth to a squeak. A squeak I'd heard before. I'd never been in this house previously, but everything was all so familiar to me, squeak included, having participated in several police raids of various residences to date in 'What's it called?'

'Cumbernauld.'

Many times, I had scaled the same type of stairs. Hitherto, I had brought numerous exact same squeaks yelping and bleating into the world. I had never been in this house, but I knew its layout like the back of my hand. And, for want of a better thing to look at and to help while away the wee hours, the by-product of one stakeout after another, I knew the back of my hand so very well. So I already knew there was closet space built behind one of the main bedroom walls. I already knew access to this was courtesy of a sliding door. Not quite a hidden door, but rather designed to blend in with the wall. Easily missed if you weren't expecting it.

When dealing with Slippy Ally's type, intent on making

themselves scarce so they weren't part of this world at all, you didn't need to be a police officer to know that this should be your first port of call. But it probably helped. Accordingly, there I was, my ear up against the 'hidden' door, listening for breathing, a sign of life. You didn't need to be a fan of Columbo or TJ Hooker, either. You just needed to be a frequenter of a Scottish New Town.

As an added bonus, a frequenter of hospital rooms too.

My body was unstable. Bones bolted together, guts knotted, sinew and tendons tied up in pretty bows. If I was to be unentangled, I'd be the jigsaw man on the River Clyde. A collection of limbs and organs, a pair of eddying eyeballs, all floating downstream but held in some gravitational field, ensuring each body part, in relation to the others, didn't stray too far from its normal position. My decapitated head floating above my torso with all the other slabs of meat following suit, following a recognisable pattern. There would be gaps, distinct, untethered, but still very much capable of forming a human shape in the water.

It was nice to be reminded of being human, at least some of the time.

I'd never had good experiences with hospitals. To be fair, who has? But in my case, the last time I was confined to a hospital bed I was attacked by a massive wild dog. The beast had snuck in undetected, along with his owner, who was something of a mad dog himself.

A Devil Dog.

Hospitals. The places that were supposed to fix and heal, what were they to do with the unhealable and unfixable? At night, darkness spooled over me like it was a quilt. It stalked me, descended on me, a coating so thin it nuzzled the ends of the hairs on my arms while knocking the breath from my lungs. The absence of heat forming droplets of air rolling down my face. I could feel it. I could sense it. I wanted to scream, if not out loud then from within, but something inside me would not let me. A counterpoint. Taking this as an invitation, the darkness ballooned around me, a reflex away from smothering and crushing the life out of me. If I was brave enough, and I could have mustered inside of me the spur to open my eyes, I could have seen the dark for what it truly was. That there was something more to it than a collection of undulating shades. That it bared a set of sharp white teeth.

My body was held in a wire cage while my grinding bones fused, as my muscles slowly atrophied. I could no longer remember what it was like to eat solid food. I had no way of measuring time, reaching the point that I had come to doubt its existence. I was less than human. Less than what it means to be human. Pain was my constant companion, but I was acclimatised to it. And when I was not in pain, I worried I was turning into someone else. I guess I just needed somebody to talk to. Someone who could help alleviate my fears, keep me calm and in the zone. Someone to talk to.

I just needed somebody to talk to who wasn't myself.

Back in Cumbernauld, I slid the door open. The door's trajectory was a little uneven as it shifted along the tracks. A little movement, a bit more, until so unveiled before me, hanging, clinging, there was all kinds of clothing. Concoctions of silk, cotton, denim and polyester. Browns, blues, and greens. Compressed arms, flat legs, matters of the waist. Men's clothes occupied one side of the wardrobe and women's clothes the other. I wouldn't say they were in perfect harmony, but in perfect synchronicity, yes to that.

And an ear. I could see an ear.

Part of me—now there's a thing, it wasn't unheard of, call it a psychiatrist's wet dream—wanted to take that ear in my teeth and bite and maybe tear off a piece, and possibly chew. I could feel that other part of me—the angry me, the bilious me, the batshit crazy me—take shape and coalesce around my chest area, forming a unique kind of pressure. A walking talking Vesuvius, ready to burst out. The part of me which threatened to turn the air blue. The part which throttled you first and asked questions later (once you got your breath back). The part of me which was bent out of shape, or you might argue, wasn't so bent out of shape after all.

I compromised. I dialled it back in one sense, and dialled it forward in another, and I reached out and grabbed the ear by the earlobe. I gave it a twist like I was a Bobbie on the Beat from the 1950s apprehending a young scallywag who'd just let the air down from the tyres of a butcher boy's bike. The ear was moving erratically, like a fish head caught on a line, but not for long. I pulled and, deferential to the law that is cause and effect, a face followed, emerging from the assorted fabrics.

'I'm really sorry.' A man's voice emanated from around the ear, which continued to bob, jerk and zigzag. A figure was forming, flattening clothing in its trajectory; a backdrop forming, consisting of a size-16 tartan skirt. His words expressed in such a way, adopting such a tone, that said to me that even though the owner of the voice had realised the error of his ways, he lacked the necessary conviction not to do it again—and again. He'd put butter on his toast, forsaking the olive oil spread, despite all those (lovely, delicious and obesity-bating) saturated fats. When push came to shove—and pull—he'd go on and on anyway, and indefinitely.

'Slippy Ally,' I said. 'You're under arrest.'

'You'll never take me alive,' Slippy Ally squeaked, head rearing up from a shirt collar that was not his own.

'A tad overdramatic,' I said.

'You think?' And with that Slippy Ally leaned back, and the world leaned back with him. In the blink of an eye and the crossing of a stitch, he was swallowed up by the contents of the wardrobe.

I still had a grip of his ear with no intention of letting go. Such were the forces at work, they contrived to lift me clean off my feet. And before I could react in any other way, I was dragged forward, and I followed Slippy Ally in.

I had a recurring dream where Dr Dawn and I would run off hand in hand. We'd run through a corridor, a tunnel, a forest, a sandy beach, clutching our respective notebooks and humming half-remembered tunes from our childhood. Our legs were like machine parts, our kneecaps knowing no limits as they threatened to pierce the heavens. We accelerated to the point our surroundings were reduced to lines and simple geometric patterns. When we stopped running, we'd see water. We had found ourselves on an island. Canary Islands, Tahiti, Fair Isle. With every dream it played out the exact same way, without deviation except for the identity of our final destination. Every time it was a different island, never to be repeated.

'I'm scared.' As I said the words, I'd turn to Dr Dawn and try to meet her gaze with my own. But her eyes danced, they'd flit bouncing from one random angle to another. It was impossible to keep up. At no point would she ever speak, and I was deprived of her deep dulcet tones. It was an imperfect dream.

Still, I was devoted to the idea of her. I was a dog and she was my owner. Someone to wag my tail at. She would hand me a bowl of dog biscuits and I would gratefully wolf them down. For all my other bodily needs, I had my IV drip. A different island, the same dream. The list of possible islands was an extensive one, but by no means infinite. It would have to end someday. And after that, what was there to do if I could no longer dream of Dr Dawn?

Oh, Dr Dawn. Through our counselling sessions, she'd made me aware of who I was and who I wasn't. What I should be and what I shouldn't be. Her deep,

deep voice. Her insightful, sometimes too insightful, questions. The way she straightened the pen in her hand, like a cat flicking its tail, before writing something down. She had done her work on me and she had said goodbye to me. And then there was a pause, and then she said goodbye to *me*.

Job done.

A raft was floating in the water, caught momentarily by the tide. I watched her as she boarded the raft. (Less boarded, more scampered.) I watched as she was cast adrift, floating on the ocean away from me. In time, she became little more than a speck on the horizon. And then a blink, and she was gone. And in her place...

There was something inside me that scuttled about. This scrabbling thing, I could feel it predominantly across my waist, my chest, but it was everywhere. Pushing up against my bones, my muscles, tiny detonations, distinct pressure points. Sometimes I was aware of tendrils which snaked up and tapped out a secret code on the inside of my throat. It coveted my brain, this scurrying creature, I was sure of it. It had enjoyed ascendancy there many times before, taking control of my mind sporadically but emphatically. How did the song go?

'A brain that is lost now, but oh so dearly held.'

It was a terrible writhing vindictive thing. Given the chance, it would toy with you before it hurt you. It would claim it existed because bad things exist, but I think this is too simplistic and unreconstructed a view. There had to be another way. There had to be more to its existence than the servicing of a reptilian article of faith.

All this time, not moving, only thinking. I was a slab of meat kept at room temperature, a white mattress on a white bed the extent of my known universe. I'd come to know that to heal was not contingent on the mere resetting of bones and healing of ligaments. Not wholly dependent on the knitting together of form and physique. It not only concerned the physical, requiring also the rewiring of the brain.

They say all roads lead to some place, so why not Cumbernauld?

I was falling. Clothes snaked around me. Emaciated trouser legs tousled my hair. Empty sleeves wrapped around my ankles. Slippy Ally was trying to give me the slip among the slips. A vortex of flailing arms and hemlines. I could taste sock in my mouth. But I couldn't give up. I had come this far. I had to give chase. To be in pursuit. It was my duty to keep reaching out, to continue grappling and, somewhere along the patterns and prints, try and catch the bad guy.

Always falling. The fear of failing.

There was something inside of me. An illness eating away at me, fighting for dominance. It was just like bamboo: if you listened carefully enough, you could hear the sound of it growing. From inside of me, you could hear the munching.

Before the fall, I'd be polishing the buttons and buckle of my uniform and I'd catch something unwelcome and unwholesome in my reflection. A personality. Something that would rather scratch my eyes out, make me look away, than let me see the truth. It had a face. It was my face. It had a name.

I wanted it out.

It should have been a simple process. For the most part, I was an open book. Even when on duty, I was careful that everything I said was done in a professional capacity. I'd say 'Have a nice day,' and that's what I was hoping for. I really hoped that you would have a nice day. When asking crowds to disperse, always mindful to put forward a more constructive alternative to rioting and ransacking the local Co-op, I'd suggest perhaps they take up pottery or learn a new language to while away the day. There were some interesting Art Therapy adult colouring books out there. There must be a jigsaw puzzle at home, box lying unopened and gathering dust on a shelf somewhere.

As a foster child, being shuttled from one family to another, the ground constantly shifting beneath my feet, I'd had no choice but to adapt. To change the only thing I could change, which was how I came across to other people. Adults mostly. My insides always remained the same. I had the same gut, the same beating heart, the same pair of lungs. But from the outside, to adapt, I needed to be one thing to one and another thing to another. To be all things to all people.

The foster families. Coteries of extremes. Some were stern, authoritarian environments for a six, seven, eight, nine, ten-year-old to be in. Scary even, choked with rules and impossible standards. Others were liberal in comparison, practically tripping over you, half forgetting you were even there. Some foster siblings, however temporary, wasted no time in resenting my presence, while others enjoyed this new ephemeral plaything just introduced to the family. Mostly, through no fault of my own, I'd spend six months tops with one family, as little as three weeks with another, before the inevitable ferrying off to pastures new. Chameleonic. Every time, I developed the ability to be what I had to be, drawing on some arcane animalistic instinct, to stand my ground if need be, or embrace any instances of kindness. Never to thrive, but be what was required to survive. Never to flourish, but to do what was necessary to prevail.

Get out with you. *Get oot wi' ye.*

An excavation was required. A coring. If only I could have willed the badness out of me, expunged the foulness, the misery, the decay. If only I could have made this possible using the power of the mind. Made it as simple as the flicking of a switch.

An exorcism.

A gaggle of nurses entered my room. They took up their pre-appointed positions around my bed. From each of their persons they removed and bundled up a black swirling mass of cloth and beads that could have passed for a nun's habit and tucked them under my mattress. They laid hands on me and talked to me in a language I didn't understand. The talking was incessant, if at times infuriatingly quiet. For all I knew they were speaking and whispering in tongues.

Water was splashed on my face; each droplet vying for every pore, frantically trying to grab my full attention. At least, I hoped it was water. My body rose up in bits. An arm was propelled in the air, followed by a hip bone, followed by the lower part of a leg. A squadron of body-shaped dirigibles, stuffed with muscle and blood rather than helium, floated in formation above my bed. So many individual body parts, all caught in each other's trajectory, it was difficult to count just how many before my eyes misted over. Dangling, held up by barely visible high-tension wires. Barely visible as in transparent. All done in the name of piecemeal levitation. A floating man. A floating jigsaw man.

My skull was overrun. My face was riven. It told of ancient stories, of one in particular. My eyes were bloodshot.

And he was back. *I was back.* Bilious and furious, exposed and malignant. A yin to some fucker's yang. A ball of overwrought anger. I was the cat's pyjamas. I was wearing the cat's pyjamas.

My lips were moving, my mouth was working. Gushing out of me, words shaped into weapons, the usual threats, the most exotic of police interrogation patois. Start by taking a confession first, and then you ask your questions.

'*Break off your jaw and use it as part of an ashtray.*'

'*Gouge out your eyes and use the empty sockets as pencil holders.*'

'*You smell of vomit, and not the good kind.*'

I looked up and saw only stars. Only the night sky. My room no longer had a ceiling. The hospital no longer had a roof. Outside, the elements had picked up and I could see, caught in the ether, tousled, tangled, almost alive, a selection of clothes flying high in the sky. Trousers, dresses, shirts, tops, scarves, all just flapping, carried as they were by the currents. The silk and cotton and polyester. They could have belonged to any ordinary couple, two perfectly ordinary citizens. The type it was my solemn duty to protect and serve and keep safe. They could have been the occupants, for example, of a perfectly ordinary egalitarian house in Cumbernauld. A Mr and Mrs Campbell, if you will. A Mr Hunt and a Mr McGhee. A Mr and Mrs MacPhellimey.

Could I take as prophecy the absence of a roof? Which would mean I was a bag of bones. Which would mean the screams of the doctors and nurses had done their work. Which would mean...

There was a heat around my midriff. There was a surge. A flare. A collection of light and explosions like a Catherine wheel lighting up the sky. All the colours along the spectrum, as far as the eye could see. The trick was to not only let it out, but also to not let it back in. The trick was to make the pain worth it. Make it all mean something.

...it was me. I screamed and I couldn't stop screaming.

I didn't want to stop screaming. It was a release.

I had a disease living inside me. A bad side, a

malignant alter ego. Something unyielding and amoral; something without compassion or restraint. Consumed by violence, unbound by law or common decency. To rip and tear and bite and snare. Something that was not me. Another person. I am me. *He was me.*

And he was gone. *I was gone.*

For the first time since I could remember I was unburdened. The growth inside me, the cocktail of carcinogens, was expelled into the air. It was driven through the open roof and propelled into the night sky where it would take its place next to the stars. Not like the sun, but something opaque, an outlier, a celestial malignancy. A dark star.

A dark star prone to shouting out a torrent of abuse at any passing Solar System bodies. *'Call yourself a meteor shower? A shower of bastards more like.'*

Back on earth, click by click, piece by piece, moveable digit by interlocking limb, I reassembled. I came together, gently rocking, chest lifting. Something slight and something empty. Floating like a feather went I, rocking to and fro, back down to bed. Arms dangling at each side, lighter than light.

And I was falling again, but this time it was different. I was looking down. Someone was looking up. A skinny face. A face not my own.

Almost bald, virtually hairless, even his eyebrows lacked motivation.

The man looking up had a twisted smile that at any moment could split open and grow, and keep growing, until it reached the breadth of a chasm. The length of a river. But there was no time, no wriggle room. All I could do was look into those wide eyes, which carried no emotion. Wide white eyes, forming a canvas. Cloudy white pools. The eyes of a shark. This time I kept on falling. This time the rest of me caught up with my falling tears. And I braced myself for the sickening thud of impact. The haemorrhaging of blood and bone that would surely follow.

'WHAT THE...'

What was that?

Whatever it was, it was lost now to the wind. Snaffled by a pair of cinnamon corduroys.

Falling into the white.

Which was what was needed.

I needed to be at my most hollow, my most exposed, before I could even think about turning things around. All this before I could even consider grasping the nettle and put myself back together again and banish the spectre of one H Dumpty.

And slowly, now I laid down to rest, incrementally, periodically, I healed.

***

Today.

I learned to walk today.

3.

Fank you

I stood and watched the ramp on the approach to Kingston Bridge. There was a sharp turn and from my vantage point you quickly lost sight of the cars once they were on the bridge. And I can only accept what I can see. My worldview does not extend to beyond what's in front of me. A white car came off the ramp, going too fast in my opinion. (It could have been white, it could have been a car, I have no recollection, but let's just go with this.) Moments before, the car did not exist. Only now, now it was there in the crosshairs, could I accept the certainty of its existence. Taking the sharp turn on the bridge would subsequently seal its fate and extinguish it from reality. My point is that it was real for the duration; the fleeting moments it occupied my line of sight. Otherwise, it was gone to me, purged from my mind, expunged from memory. I did not wake up one morning and decide I would have such a limited and potentially debilitating worldview. That's just the way it is.

I am a lazy speaker. I pronounce 'th' as 'f'. I took a cold call some time ago. The girl on the other side asked me an array of personal questions and I was hesitant and evasive and I could not work out what she was trying to tell me or sell to me and eventually all I could say was 'fank you.' She responded in a shrill voice. She asked me 'why?'

I wrote it down, so it must have been true.

Thank you. Fank you. Fuck you.

She must have thought I'd said 'Fuck you' which was ridiculous. Why would I say such a thing? But the connection on the phone went click and the incoming phone number was hidden, and I wouldn't have had the confidence or gumption to phone back anyway, leaving no chance of clarification or correction. So, the phrase underwent a metamorphosis, a conversion of letters and sound, and it became 'fuck you.' I'd said 'fuck you.' I'd responded to a faceless voice, which only existed for the length of a meaningless phone call, with a 'fuck you.' What could I have done about it? What could anyone have done about it, including Jesus?

I wore a balaclava over my head. There was the smell of diesel and petrol in the air. It *was* the air. I breathed it in as best I could and I walked to a street in Tradeston. Or at least that was the presumption. Sometimes I lost track. I'd have no memory of how I got from there to here, but such a condition was of little concern to me. It had its advantages, removing the tedium of travel. It released me from the unrelenting humdrum of displacement from A to B. I would go as far as to consider it a blessing. A blurring.

Blue. The colour was blue. A purple blue plumage. Imprinted on the blue, block capitals in emboldened white took shape, a tell-tale lexicon which read *Army & Navy Surplus*. The front of the building looked like it had been sculpted from rock. It was a gateway. The stuff of odyssey, of ritualistic intent. Of mythmaking. I wrote the address down on a Post-it.

Clutching a Bag for Life, durable, reusable, stitched in a way as to make it weight bearing, I entered. Inside, I was greeted by rows of racks of clothes. A jungle of battle green trousers, camouflage jackets, grey blue jumpers with epaulettes on the shoulders, boots for giants. The scene was so vivid, I swear I could hear the shots being fired, the shouts of the oppressor, the screams of pain of the oppressed. There were so many trapped souls inside this place, dedicated to the snuffing out of others, even if this meant dying themselves. It was all mad; all mad...

At the far end of the shop, I approached the man behind the counter. I did so in the knowledge I would not ask for his name, nor would he volunteer it. He was looking straight at me, but still, I felt it necessary to announce my presence with a cough.

'Morning,' he said. 'Or is it afternoon, surely it's not evening?'

'That's some cough you got on you, man,' he said.

'You going skiing?' he said, referring to the balaclava wrapped around my face, three oval slits over eyes and mouth the only indication that a man of indeterminate age lurked inside. 'You don't have to wear a mask no more, not if you don't want to.'

'No,' I said, unsure which of his questions I was answering. If any.

'That's not a bother,' he said. 'You see something you like?' The man, in his fifties, with his back unnaturally straight which made me think perhaps he was ex-army, continued without taking a breath. 'Let me show you this,' he said and from behind the counter he took out a steel-plated waistcoat. He then proceeded, with no lack of enthusiasm, to slam the waistcoat down onto the panelled beech wood surface. The clang of metal bounced around the shop interior. 'Just in, flak jacket all the way from Iraq. Tell you what, I'll throw in some genuine bullet holes for free.'

I was patient. I kept my counsel. I was content to wait. To wait until the man behind the counter finished his elaborate sales pitch. To wait until the day the River Clyde freezes over. To wait until the last human was feasting on the bones of a former lover. Instead, I focussed on the black wool of the balaclava on my face which insulated and united me. It was an extension of me. The mask was me. Without it I was something else. Something which did not exist.

'Roy Lichtenstein sent me,' I said.

At this, the man tensed up and came to attention. He looked around him several times, checking that no prying sets of eyes were in the vicinity. He did so until satisfied that the coast was clear. 'Ah, you'll be wanting army surplus then. The *real* army surplus. Why didn't you say? Spend over a grand, there's a 10% discount...'

I had no money. I think he knew that already without me having to explain. I think he liked to humour people that way.

I was in a side room, or a back room. I had no recollection of how I got there, but I refused to mourn such lost moments. For moments it must have been, because I was still inside the shop, albeit ensconced in a room. It was a secret room, a fact it was welcome to. Mounted on each of the four walls were all kinds of weaponry: Bazookas, rifles, an ArmaLite, revolvers, pistols, grenades, a Claymore sword, bayonets, hunting knives. Originating from China, America, Switzerland, Balmedie. Up on brackets, all ducks in a row. Combined, they made for a glittering prize, even though the room was devoid of windows and natural sunlight.

'Fank you,' I said.

'Ah,' the man from the counter said, looking down and rearranging his feet. He had half a smile on his face. I couldn't read the other half of his expression. 'Fuck you too.'

4.

Dream of Tannoch

I had a hole inside me, one I did not want to be filled. Or healed. I had no memories or recollection of my other self. I couldn't swear that such things weren't hidden away somewhere, in the deeper recesses, lurking within the shadows, lost among the grey matter, but I had no intention of going looking for them. I was sure I was diminished in some people's eyes, now I was incomplete, now I had lived only half a life. But not in my mind.

Really, I should be floating on air. I was liberated, I was free. How could I be blamed for any of his actions, now he was dead? I was a free man, yes, but trapped in a broken body. A blank sheet, but a crumpled blank sheet.

Nor was I content at stopping things there. There was more on the checklist. Things to change, to have changed, various goals moving around my pixelized brain like a hungry Pac-Man. I was determined. A steam train rattling along the tracks. An elemental force of white smoke and pistons.

Take dreams, for example. Dreams are funny. Frankly, I had no time for them. Or so I had decided, as if it was that simple for the conscious mind to decide on such things and just as easily turn dreams off. Reality for me had become so fractured and irregular, my waking life was already punctured and spiky. I was transformed from good cop and bad cop to barely half a cop, exiled to a hospital bed. Given all this, what could dreams offer me? What could they bring to the table?

The operating table.

Dreams confined to exotic islands and Dr Dawn, drifting away from me into the horizon, into the sunset. Now she was gone, nothing could ever take the place of that. Nothing that was any good.

Jumbled dreams. Mixed up. Messed up. Dreams of why we dream.

Maybe this was why I dreamt of Tannoch after all this time. Perhaps, but I could still ask who decides these types of things? Why put myself through that much upset, that much trauma, especially having suppressed it for so long? If it was a question worth asking then I've always said, you should ask it. Ask away, ask it many, many times. Ask it while standing in a wide-open field, situated in...

'What's it called?'

There was the kerfuffle of birds chirping, but the

hubbub originated from too far off to form anything more meaningful than background fuzz. Away from the birdsong, closer, occupying my line of sight, was wire fencing pressed against a line of overgrown bushes and stunted trees. A notice attached to the fence announced '*Danger Deep Water*'. I wanted to get closer to the fence and see for myself just how deep the water was but something inside me—a warning voice, dark and problematic, consisting of scraping static, as far away from birdsong as one can possibly get—told me that if I did, I'd never be able to pull away again. I wouldn't have to fall into the currents to be dragged under. Dreams are full of warnings and messages. But, in a way, so what? The fact of whether you heed or listen or react to dreams is already preordained. Set in stone. Written in the stars. There were no real choices, only the illusion of choice. And not far away from this, a hop, skip and a jump, were the stables.

No choice but to move and twist my feet and distil the impression of movement. The scene altered around me—the air shifted as well—and this time I was standing in the police stables in Tannoch, located in...

'*What's it called?*'

There was damp in the air, but mostly situated at my back. The smell of horseshit wasn't so overbearing that it cancelled out the other smells of cut grass and sweat. There was a lack of natural light, but I was aware of the shapes of several horses, each occupying a separate box stall. Something had agitated them. They were kicking, stamping, trying to turn in too confined an area. The source of their distress could have been down to my sudden appearance, but this seemed unlikely. I was dressed in a uniform that would have been familiar to them. I was with the mounted unit then, in my previous life, my professional life, which ended fifteen years ago. Shifting from Blairfield Farm to Tannoch, before negotiating the turning on the road which took me on the path to becoming a police detective. This was a life where I carried their scent, where I smelled of horses.

When you work with horses, the expectation is that you spend just as much time with them when you're not working. You groom them, you feed them, whisper quiet words of encouragement in their ear. It's all about establishing relationships, becoming comfortable with each other. Over one and a half metres tall, a metric ton of toned muscle. If you do your job right, out on the streets, you've got yourself an equine version of the Batmobile.

This was what made the discovery all the more shocking.

'What's it called? Cumbernauld.'

I reached out to the horse closest to me. Its pelt was white with black spots. In the dark, while I waited for my sight to adjust, you could mistake the markings for gaping holes. I held my hand out a foot or so from the animal, allowing it to acclimatise to my arrival. My action had the desired calming effect and I gave its snout a wee pat.

'What's so wrong?' I said, my voice hushed. 'What's spooking you?'

The horse breathed out nasally and noisily. This appeared to start a chain reaction among the other horses in the stable. A series of fluttering, flappy exhalations passing from one horse to another. The stamping of hooves. There was one exception at the far end of the stable. Located there was the absence of upset, of disturbance. There was another sound, a lighter sound, but persistent all the same. It was a drip. A continuous drip.

I focussed on the drip in the dimness. I let it guide me. Even in the dark, there appeared before me an even darker shape. A horse's head was leaning down, seeping blood. Only the stable hatch was keeping its frame from collapsing wholly to the ground.

I grabbed the head, clutching it where the mane should have been. I lifted it, most of its bulk still pressed up against the hatch but a dead weight all the same, so I could have a better look. My grip held, even though it was slick and slimy to the touch, squirming up between the gaps in my fingers. Skull and bone still retaining a recognisable shape. Dripping blood forming perfectly straight lines, never crisscrossing. The horse's face had been skinned. Taken clean off.

Horse blood gathered in my hand, but despite my best efforts I could not release it. I could not let it go. All there was to do was wait for the dream to end, but still I was asking the question, why now? My alter ego was gone, exorcised, having been banished one bracing tumultuous night, I was sure of that, but something else was stirring in its place. Nature and vacuums. A feeling. A dead, skinned feeling. A funny feeling.

Why dream of Tannoch after all this time? Wasn't this funny timing? A funny dream, as in funny peculiar? It was a question worth asking.

5.

Party Fears Two

I was aware of a laptop on a coffee table, top flipped open and its screensaver on. I was more than aware; it was me who put it there. A Ford Gran Torino, tomato red with white stripes, adorned the screen. The Gran Torino was stationary, but like a caged animal, defying the two dimensions that sought to bind it, its engine threatened to unshackle and roar into life. I liked to think that I could look away at any time and return my gaze only to see the car tear up a chunk of digitised tarmac, back tyres turning like spinning plates, in the process of speeding off-screen. Most of the time I liked to entertain the idea, but not so much today.

The Gran Torino screensaver hid a multitude of sins. When I got pissed one night, to give an example, I gave in to one alcohol-fuelled impulse too many and joined the Patrick Stewart fan club online. This one stayed with me though, as I still check for updates sometimes. I suppose so I could think about him some more. I'd even read the odd article posted on the website. A video recital of Shakespeare's sonnets. A blow-by-blow blog account of a lunch date with Sir Ian McKellen. His public forgiving of James Corden for being, well, James Corden. All reasonably above board, but then again there was the night I spent staring at a topless photo of him. I was drinking wine at the time. I think I was trying to find hairs on his chest, sure in the knowledge that he didn't have any on his head. I never found a hair, not one, no matter how many times I went back to look.

There was no wine to accompany my latest venture—it was too early in the day—which involved filling out a form online. Part of an effort of introducing some spice into my life. Maybe even, dare I say it, a little romance.

I hadn't got very far. It didn't take long before I was thinking *Whoa, that's a little intrusive.* But taking a step back helped me reconsider whether asking for my favourite colour was *that* intrusive. Did red with white stripes count as a bona fide colour? It was hopeless. It was pointless. And part of me was thinking it was just as necessary. I'd entered my name as Julie Spencer. It seemed wrong to omit the 'DS' from up front. I felt exposed by this somehow, incomplete, pared down. It didn't take a genius (which is just as well) to come to the conclusion that such a thought—the latest in a long line of many—couldn't be considered healthy or desirable. All the more reason to kickstart my life, I reckoned, and return with renewed gusto to the online form.

The mustering of sufficient enthusiasm was a work in progress, so the intention was to take a break from the tyranny of the coffee table and make myself a cup of tea. I'd been drinking lots of tea recently, mostly as an alternative to drinking lots of coffee.

I'd been on my feet for five minutes all told, but I hadn't left the living room. Instead, I hovered over the solid oak mantelpiece where I counted repeatedly in my head the number of sympathy cards there, forming a row of nervy, hunched journeymen intent on delivering their message, then keeping themselves to themselves. To be fair, one read was all it took.

Our hearts go out to you in your time of sorrow.

Thinking of you at this time of loss.

Our sincere condolences.

Everything was still numb and I was conscious I hadn't started to grieve yet. It was important to try to feel something, to go as far as force something out of me, but no, there was nothing. Instead, I repeated the phrases from the cards in my head, as well intentioned and vacuous as they were. On a whim, I took out the natural spaces between the words, crunched them together so they formed a tapered loop.

Our hearts go out toyouinyourtimeofsorrow.

It was obvious to me I couldn't put it off forever. All the arguments against seeing him on constant rotation, occupying my overheated cranium, slowly turning me doolally. It wasn't as if seeing him could make things any worse, could it? I was already climbing the walls.

Thinking of you atthistimeofloss.

If I waited it out any longer, I might have left it too late. If what I was hearing was true, the miracle of surviving the fall was now in danger of being usurped by the prospect of the miracle of a complete recovery. It played on my fear of finally deciding to go, only to find him already discharged from hospital. I just needed to see him with my own eyes. To prove, to myself more than anything, that I could frame him in a different way. To give him a proper identifiable shape. A living, breathing presence. One that could comfortably exist outside of my head.

Oursincerecondolences.

***

'Why didn't you wake me?' he said.

I stood there in his room, having settled on doing the right thing and let him sleep. For the main, I was re-acclimatising, after a short break, to the fractured sterile ritual that comes at you with a hospital visit. You couldn't impose your personality on a hospital, it imposed itself on you. You were aware of everything, the corridors, the ceilings, the weight of the doors, like you were discovering these things for the first time, even though nothing had changed since your last visit. Or since any visit.

Eventually, he opened his eyes. He was more awake and alert than I could ever have expected from him.

He wasted no time in asking me a question. 'You were sleeping,' went the answer.

He sat up. He needed to use a combination of the pulley positioned above the bed and one of the raised sides as leverage, but he did it. He grunted, body shaking a little; there were beads of perspiration forming on his brow. I couldn't help but stare in awe as the whole simple act played out in front of me; I was only human. And that was the point, so was he, allegedly. The carrying out of such a perfunctory act by a body so ruined and broken was nothing short of phenomenal. Miraculous, for want of another overused word.

'So, what brings you round these parts, DS Spencer?' His shoulders tensed, his back unnaturally straight, like he was fighting the beginnings of a coughing fit.

'I was in the neighbourhood,' I said.

He was swallowing furiously, his Adam's apple a bouncing ball. There was a clock ticking somewhere. There was a question inside of me I'd need to let out. The hospital walls were closing in. Those familiar, so unfamiliar, walls. The room was spinning. I couldn't trust the floor beneath my feet. But this was all delaying the inevitable, and the truth will out.

I said to him, 'I need to know if you're planning on coming back?'

***

My body was a series of negotiations. My breathing

was an obstacle course. And I was crossing the balancing beam, slogging through the mud, and running around the traffic cones. I had to try and stabilise matters as I waited for everything to fall back into place, and a kind of mental and physical joined-up thinking to impose itself. I had to wait for the heat in my chest, the pain in my sides, the heaviness of my lungs, and the beating of my tell-tale heart to recede, in order to become a working human again. It was the least I could do, I had company.

My pillow had twisted and crept up on me, so it was still supporting my back but in a skew-whiff, corkscrew kind of way. On reflection, all the huffing and puffing and straining and groaning had the beneficial impact of cutting down the usual chit-chat expected of social visits. My inability to join in conversation, albeit temporarily, prompted her to get straight to the point. 'I need to know if you're planning on coming back?' she said.

'Soon,' I said. The sound of my voice was uneven, but she got the gist. 'Soon as I'm ready, fingers crossed, the doctors say my recovery is nothing short of...'

'Miraculous,' she said, her own voice barely registering above a whisper. But a whisper not made of awe. It was flat. It seemed to come from a sense of disappointment. A cloth that had been wrung out. Which was fair enough, no complaints from me. I wasn't expecting a standing ovation.

She seemed to process the ramifications of what I had said pretty quickly. Her expression changed from consternation to something more neutral. She approached the bed. 'Do you mind,' she said and reached over to knead and straighten the pillow allegedly supporting my back. Despite the need for adjustment, forward then back, it didn't hurt a bit. Maybe there was hope for me after all. For the first time in a long time, maybe it was okay to feel human.

'Thank you,' I said.

'Can I sit?' she said, motioning at the plastic chair adjacent to the bed.

'Of course.' I tried to smile, but I couldn't feel my teeth inside my mouth so I couldn't trust that my lips were doing the right thing.

She sat and lowered her head to the point she was staring at the floor. She touched her nose at regular intervals using the same finger.

'You're a legend now,' she said. 'They call you Lazarus back at the station. You've been called it so many times, the name has lost the irony it once might have had. You want to come back, the Super will fall over himself to welcome you with open arms. It'll be a fist pumping, elbow bumping frenzy.'

'You're the poster boy,' she said. Her voice was as flat as a pancake, which said, *you might be their poster boy, but you sure as hell ain't my poster boy.*

'That was never my intention,' I said.

It wasn't that long ago she wanted to report me for misconduct. Challenging my suitability as Detective Inspector. *A defective detective.* As partners, part of a team, we were always chalk and cheese, working on cases together, coming at things from different perspectives. I was the calm one, she was the fiery one, but I never thought it would end so messily between her and me, so acrimoniously. But *it wasn't that long ago* equated to a lifetime ago and somewhere along the way, in light of recent events, like the unwavering flow of water, I was happy to let bygones be bygones.

I was the calm one…

For the moment, though, what was more pressing was the desire to cough. But I knew the resultant pain would cut a swathe through my chest and abdomen. It would rip me in two, so I fought against the compulsion with all my might and, mercifully, I willed it gone. A need of words to fill the vacuum created by a lost cough. 'I know…' I said, 'I know we've not always seen eye to eye. I could have been more open with you. I've always admired you DS…'

At this, she raised her head and put up a hand to get me to stop. It was clear why. We'd both got what we wanted out of the conversation already. She was different, had acquired a harder edge since last we talked. There were lines on her face, hardly noticeable, but there all the same, should you take the time to study it long enough. But I couldn't leave it there.

'I was sorry to hear about your mother,' I said.

She did not flinch, did not react. It was as if grief was not only inside her, it surrounded her like oxygen. She couldn't acknowledge it, give it more credence or legitimacy, not when it pressed against her skin, not when it resided in the marrow of her bones. But despite the intensity of it all, and maybe because of this, I was sure her grief would reach its peak soon. Not until then could things subside, by tiny amounts at first, but even here I was hopeful there'd be room for other things. For other emotions. A reconciliation, perhaps, of sorts.

'Is there anything I can get for you?' she said eventually, her frame still and statuesque; her lips not appearing to be moving.

'Yes, tea please,' I said. 'I'd love a cup of tea.'

***

The DI stared at the little card cup which I'd managed to tease out of a vending machine situated near the hospital reception. He did so with a look of something akin to horror. A deflated teabag on a hook floated in the sheepishly hot water. It was like something had died in the cup, a floating body, stone cold. He blew on the tea, watching the surface swill, which seemed to pacify him a little. He curled his lips, and there I was expecting to see fangs. Instead, his head dipped. A first sip was pronounced with a protracted slurp.

That done, he said, 'Thank you.'

Having returned to my seat, I sat on my hands and marvelled at his ability to even take the cup unaided. A split second before, his hand was trembling from the wrist up, only for the shaking to stop emphatically at the point of contact. And I was thinking, what was the point of such a display? Was he trying to impress me? Or was he so looking forward to a cup of any kind of tea that flowing from this came a steely determination not to spill a drop? Maybe it was both. It was a possibility. And why was I reading so much into this, anyway? I didn't know what to think.

How could he even consider going back to work? To the job? After what I'd seen—after what he knew I'd seen? He was one man with two faces. He was a monster. He didn't care. There was always an inner calm about him, but it was wafer-thin, hiding something darker. Embryonic thin. And yet, how did I feel, now I'd actually seen him? Having convinced myself to go and see him? I just needed him to answer the question, and say one thing or the other, and I needed to hear it for myself.

He was still the same, but still he had changed. He took a further sip, then held out the cup, faltering at first, motioning for me to take it from him. I pinched my nose momentarily, an involuntary movement, before leaning forward. I reached out and all of a sudden it felt like I was taken back in time.

It was only a short while ago, a period of time worthy of the label déjà vu. I was in another hospital room reaching out to a different person, someone much older, much closer to me, but as a result of her illness more of a stranger all the same. Where I needed my wits about me to fight back the urge to call out her name, to bite my bottom lip, to shake her and ask her, demand of her, who she thought I was. And demand she acknowledge what she means to me in return. It was far too late for any of that.

I realised then, climbing my way out of the vines, the bracken of my thoughts, that he was staring at me. Like I was the floating dead teabag. Like I was stone cold.

'Funny you being here, DS Spencer,' he said. 'I don't mean to be rude,' he added quickly. 'Now I think about it, you are possibly the last person on earth I would expect to be here right now. Funny, I mean, as in funny peculiar.'

I nodded slowly. His words, his tone seemed genuine to me, irritatingly so.

'Funny, DI,' I said, at least half in agreement. 'As in funny, funny.'

6.

Still Life

I was cured. I no longer slept with a hammer under my pillow. They had healed me of that at least.

'A car is waiting for you,' the nurse said.

It was indeed. The issue at hand, though, was how to exit the building.

'Crutches or wheelchair?' he said.

I was still tall and thin, but after recent events and long months of recovery, a little more malnourished. And even though I had been explicit in my request that no one should meet me—I would come to them—it seemed pretty obvious the expectation from the hospital at least was that I choose one of crutches or wheelchair. Leaving the building on my own steam wasn't an option, apparently. The hospital staff had done so much for me to get me this far, such dedication and not a little patience, I would not dare to complain.

'Crutches,' I said. 'Thank you.'

The nurse handed me a brace of crutches like the passing of ceremonial swords in a character-building episode of *Game of Thrones*. I swung each crutch simultaneously, vertically to the floor and like the legs of R2D2 they nestled on either side. Instantaneously, they had become part of me, an extra pair of appendages to call my own. I lifted my feet to demonstrate the crutches could take my weight. I was impeccably balanced, a man in effortless tandem with sticks of aluminium.

'Very good,' the nurse said. He smiled at me. A tired smile I thought. 'You're good to go.'

'Thank you,' I said. 'Thanks to everyone. I can't thank all of you enough. Thank you.'

The nurse's gaze dropped. I'd been the centre of attention for so long, all consuming, occupying both him and his fellow nurses and doctors; the jigsaw man consisting of so many pieces all requiring meticulous assembly. But that was then, and now he had moved on. I'd need follow-up physiotherapy and had been referred to Police Rehabilitation (I had their number), but clearly it was time for me to move on as well.

I said, 'What's the weather like?' I was already on the move, one crutch swinging after another, a series of staccato movements, limbs like springs continually requiring to be wound up.

'Tousy,' the nurse said, but not to my recently departed face. The word followed me downwind so to speak, or more accurately down corridor. Tousy wasn't a meteorological term I was familiar with, but I was willing to go with it.

The front doors of the hospital opened in obeyance to my encroaching, erratic, cog turning movement. Taking advantage of the gap caused by the sliding doors, I whirled through. Outside, a whoosh of wind greeted me. It played with my hair.

A silver Kia Picanto, driven by a plain-clothes officer called Doug, lay in wait in the car park on the far side of the hospital grounds. It was just a case of shuffling out and making myself known to him. I'd go as far as to embrace the task and, without further ado, venture out further into the fresh air.

The very fresh air.

The wind whipped up, suddenly doubling its efforts, and a whirling cyclone of invisible whippets set upon me from all directions. I withstood the buffeting as best I could. My joints stretched, my muscles tightened, taking the strain with each treacherous gust. The wind was howling in my ears and I bared my teeth in response. I hung on to my crutches for dear life, determined not to be toppled over by the gale. This wasn't in the script. This was meant to be a new start, not a hoary dreich retread of 'man versus the Scottish weather'.

A gust hit me square in the chest, but I refused to give ground. Never to retreat. There was no way I was going back through those sliding doors, now behind me. I hadn't lost all of my gumption. I still had my drive. I still had myself.

I juddered to and fro, me and my two new pals either side of me. I was jostled out and in, bullied by the wind, making me look like a badly coordinated mime of an amateur skier. However, I still deemed the hurly-burly acceptable, it was something I could gladly tolerate. I closed my watering eyes and searched inside me for a sign and found something assured and pristine. The perfect contrast to the tumult all around me, an inner calm. I was fine with it.

Something so right and so strong.

It was all good.

7.

Balaclava

Was it tomorrow or was it later today? Both could be a possibility, it depended on one's point of reference. Ultimately, though, it did not matter. Did Moses stem the Flood by arguing it was a Tuesday instead of a Monday?

As of now, a Ford Focus, the type customised by Strathclyde police, was parked in a street. Not the street I required them to be in, but I wanted those inside the car to be real people. I owed them that, so I had them talk. I had them say something like this—

PC sat in the front passenger seat. 'You should come out wif me sometime,' he said.

WPC was behind the wheel. 'Honestly?' she said. 'Wif you, PC? Can ah claim overtime?'

'Come on, WPC, you're always complaining you don't have anyone to go out wif,' PC said. Subconsciously, he began to flick the police radio attached to the front of his uniform with his index finger. He liked to engage in banter to dispel the boredom that made up much of the working day. The waiting for something, the reporting of a crime, the only certainty lying in the knowledge that it was bound to happen eventually. That's all it was, all it boiled down to, although who knows how he'd react if WPC reciprocated in kind.

'Ah have plenty of people to go out wif,' she said. 'Only the other day ah had to turn down Brad Pitt because ah'd already arranged a night out of gin and Pimm's wif Angelina Jolie.'

'And there was me finking you like a man in uniform,' he said.

WPC laughed at this. Her fellow officer could verge on the insufferable at times, but in amongst the dross there was the odd gem to be found. When finding herself in a generous mood, she'd even claim it was enough to justify the constant verbal diarrhoea.

'Calling all available units.' PC's police radio suddenly came alive. The crackly, leaden voice continued, 'Incident reported, locus of 137 Shawlands Drive.'

PC was looking at WPC. WPC was looking at PC. They both blinked. The risk of escalation into a full blinking contest wasn't far off.

'You going to answer that?' WPC said eventually.

More moments passed like stretched elastic before the car sped off, police siren splitting the firmament. And then, like the turning of a page of a pop-up book, the car arrived at its destination, swerving to a stop next to a tenement building on Shawlands Drive. The tenement was a broad, uniform building, several floors high, but ultimately, given this was the city of Glasgow, not the tallest.

Not the tallest, but PC and WPC needed to be wary of what was happening on the ground floor.

Earlier, a dog walker, doing what dog walkers do, while walking past, heard, then reported a woman's scream. I know this to be true.

'Ah don't hear anyfing,' PC said, standing presently outside the building. 'Do we go in?'

WPC flashed PC a look. It was a look that said he'd just asked the most momentously stupid question she had ever heard. No words of reply were spoken by her. None were necessary.

They moved inside and were met by a long corridor with walls of cracked whitewashed grey. Strip lighting struggled to make much of an impression beyond illuminating the mid-section of the ceiling. Immediately to their left were stone steps which led to additional floors of more of the same. To the right, several feet ahead, was the door to Flat number 1/1, which showed signs of being forced open. A force of nature was at work here.

WPC took the lead with PC following, however reluctantly, in her wake. Leading with the proximal joint of her index finger she half-knocked, half-nudged open the damaged door. The Yale lock was hanging perilously loose at an angle. WPC ghosted past the door, not waiting for a response to her knocking, while PC held back, remaining outside.

'Hullo?' Now inside, WPC walked towards another open door, this one leading from the hall into the living room. She peered in. Inside, there was a woman hunched down, bent at the knees, huddling in the corner.

'He kicked in the door,' the woman said. Her voice was clear despite the underlying shudder of panic. She wanted every word to be understood. 'He had a knife. He had some paper. He jabbed at his arm to show how sharp it was. Ah couldn't see blood, but ah believed him. He told me to scream.'

The eyes of WPC darted in all directions. She was taking in the room, simultaneously alert to any possible movement from in front of her and behind her. 'Is he still in the flat?'

'No. Ah don't know. Ah don't fink so.'

There was shouting originating from outside. WPC turned and ran back into the hall. In perpetual motion, she bolted out the front door. She re-joined the PC. He was at her side. He was retreating. His hands were thrashing, swatting away a swarm of imaginary flies. He was shouting something barely comprehensible.

'...nade,' he shrieked.

WPC stopped dead in her tracks.

'...omb,' he howled.

In their own way, both did well to react, the futility of their actions not fully dawning on them. There was something rolling on the floor. A metal egg.

There was an explosion.

She took most of the blast. The worst of it. All time stopped as WPC was transformed from a bold, purposeful, and complete human into a red wave of frayed body parts.

There were plumes of smoke, a never-ending procession. The blast had bitten a hole out of the concrete floor. There was no sign of the PC.

It was time for me to step out of the shadows, untouched by the dappled strip lighting which miraculously still shone in its flickering, diminished way. The shadows which congregated at the far end of the hall.

I stepped forward clutching my Bag for Life in one hand. I caught a glimpse of the face of WPC—it was not my main focus—floating, detached, like a decayed jellyfish. There was no life in her eyes. There were no eyes. The jaw was missing. I tried my best to excise the image from my mind, knowing that even if I failed it would not matter soon enough. I just had to move on, and her suspended corpse had to remain where it was. I focussed on the smoke.

'Cairns...' a voice said, very faint. It came not too far from where I was standing and unmistakeably it was his voice now. 'Ruth...'

Even though his comrade in arms had taken most of the blast, there was sufficient radius to cause the PC to fold in an untidy heap; his right leg extended at a funny angle. There were several tears in his uniform, each leaking blood.

His hands were the colours of bruises, but his face was mercifully untouched.

'Oh fuck,' he said. 'Ruth, stay with me. Just talk to me.'

'She's gone,' I said. I dropped the Bag for Life to the floor. In my other hand was a Jackal Classic hunting knife. 'Your voice, it's not what ah imagined it to be, not in mah head.'

Blood trickled unevenly from his mouth. I was struck by the inevitability of his real voice fading from memory and there would only be my version left. I leaned down and pressed on his chest, careful not to exert too much pressure, just enough, and I could feel the air leave his body, never to be replaced. I withdrew my hand, and then came down the knee.

'Worked it all out beforehand,' I said. The knife had a serrated edge and it was sharp. I could put it to the test. It could cut through smoke. 'Your voice. Your face.'

His chest inflated, inexplicably, surprising me. It was a last stand to upset my balance, not enough to knock me over, and I stayed true. My head was twitching.

I rested the blade on the side of his face before settling on where to make the first slice.

'Ah imagined your face,' I said.

8.

Date No. 1

I got there early, even though I didn't fancy the prospect of sitting on my own. Waiting. Waiting for a dark-haired stranger, one I'd only seen previously in black-and-white. I'd been to Six by Nico on Argyle Street before, but never on a first date. A blind date. I wasn't even sure if it was a date. I suppose I'd have to see how the meal went first before I could be certain, one way or the other. The booking was for a taster menu, six courses, and I hoped none of the dishes would be particularly messy.

The interior of the restaurant was all wood, fresh wood furnishings, designer wood. A girl who looked fourteen showed me to my table. The table, next but one to the window, was reassuringly square and designed to seat two. I sat in the chair with its back facing the far wall. Another member of the waiting staff appeared and started to fill my glass with water.

I watched as she poured and thought about ordering a bottled beer, but I didn't want to come across as too comfortable, not this early in the evening. I thanked her while attempting to conceal the effort required to force out a smile, which immediately made me feel self-conscious. And such were the shifting sands around me, there he was suddenly standing in front of me, being shown to his chair by the fourteen-year-old from earlier.

He looked at me like he'd known me forever. The photo I'd put online had me in a black top and black pair of jeans. The same clothes, it occurred to me, as I was wearing right now.

'Hi,' he said. 'I'm Robert, short for Bob.' He took off his coat in one movement to reveal a long-sleeved crew neck top. He was wearing virtually all-black as well. His trousers were charcoal grey. For some reason, I found myself imagining what he'd be like in a Christmas jumper.

'Julie,' I said, 'How are you?' I realised he had cracked a joke, but too late for me to react safely without coming over as potentially unhinged, so came to the decision to let the moment go. He looked ordinary: ordinary face, ordinary hair, ordinary mouth. That's maybe why I agreed to meet him in the first place. He was about my age, a little younger maybe. A full head of hair. I wanted to imagine him as bald, but that would also involve visualising him as an eighty-year-old and that was too much effort for one encounter. A full head of hair was fine and furthermore, nothing to suggest the formation of a mullet had to count as a bonus.

'I'm fine,' he said. 'It's stopped raining.'

'That's great.' I wasn't aware it had started raining, never mind stopped, but I knew in a 'first date' capacity any opening gambit was always going to be strained, bordering on excruciating. This was much worse than any police procedural, because I knew at some point, here among the wood panelling, I might find it necessary to reveal a piece of myself.

Each course followed a single theme. In this case it was *The Alps*. When I thought of the Alps I thought of snow-encrusted mountains with a solitary goat standing near the top of a rocky cliff face, chewing a bunch of dandelions. As the waiter explained, each course represented both the icy peaks of Chamonix and the splendour of Mont Blanc, so really, I wasn't that far off.

I chose the regular menu and he chose the vegetarian option. Maybe I'd read from his dating profile that he was vegetarian. I prided myself on remembering the details, but only in the context of looking for inconsistencies in witness statements, scrambling for anything that might lead to determining the guilt of a perpetrator, less so when it came down to an ordinary person's likes and dislikes, their lifestyle choices, the day-to-day stuff. Ordinary in the sense that no heinous crime was committed, unless the crime was looking for companionship, the search for a kindred spirit. Partners in crime together.

'Morrissey,' I said, trying to get my thought processes back on an even keel. 'Good vegetarian? Bad vegetarian?'

The question was left hanging in the air. Not one of my finest. In the nick of time, I was rescued by the serving of the first course. Raclette Fondue. An oversized plate was put in front of me accommodating an undersized serving of Crispy Pigs Head. The same sized plate was put in front of Robert. He had Salt Baked Beetroot.

Robert hunched and half-smiled in a way that suggested he might at one point in the evening work his way up to a full one. Maybe he'd intended a full smile all along, up to the point he thought better of it. 'Just vegetarian,' he said, before devouring his beetroot. I think I only counted two chews.

As for me, I sliced and dispersed and finally ate the baked cuboid offering on my plate. 'Crispy Pigs Head, this feels a lot like cannibalism,' I said, knowing that if he didn't get the joke, or worse was offended by it, then there wasn't much hope for us moving forward.

He put down his knife and fork, beetroot extinguished, and looked me straight in the eye, and laughed. It was a short laugh, which came out mostly through the nose, little more than a snort really, but a laugh was still a laugh. All in all, it was difficult to judge, and I wasn't sure why I had to rush to judgment so early in the evening anyway. Force of habit I suppose, but I was thinking this wasn't the worst of starts.

For our second course I had Salmon, he had Pumpkin. Next course in, our worlds converged as we were both served Barbecue Broccoli, Alpine Walnut and Reblochon Cheese.

I said, 'Where are you from?'

'You mean where was I brought up?' he said. 'Busby.'

'Stewarton,' I said.

There followed some silence. Not necessarily an uneasy one, nor something I could blame on the broccoli, walnut and cheese. He looked like he was happy to draw out the lack of chat a little longer, me less so.

'Do you ski?' I said, acknowledging the Alpine theme which connected the courses.

'Not really,' he said, 'I don't like snow.'

'You don't like snow?'

'Afraid not. Sorry.'

The conversation was in danger of petering out with three courses still to go. He still hadn't asked a question, not really, and if this was about to change, it rested on the one thing. The elephant in the room. Of any room I happened to be in. Or car for that matter.

'How long have you been with the police?' he said.

'Over ten years,' I said. 'I was a uniformed officer on the beat, up and down the streets from dusk to dawn, or that's how I remember it, for nearly five of them, before working up to detective sergeant.'

He smirked at this. A scarcely legible pursing of the lips, but a smirk was a smirk. I could have asked him what part of what I had just said merited such a gnarly, mean-spirited reaction. But to ask would be to show to care. And I'd decided even before this that I didn't care.

'Must be really interesting,' he said, oblivious to any hint of upset caused.

We were served the same dish again for course number four—Hen of the Woods Mushroom—but as living, breathing people we could hardly be less on the same page. I watched him cut into the mushroom's white flesh.

'Busby,' I said, 'I'll tell you about a case in Busby. A man, he could have been called Robert, perhaps short for Bob much like yourself. I don't remember all the details. But after twenty-five years of marriage, one day he got out of bed, had cornflakes for breakfast, then he strangled his wife.'

A slice of mushroom, impaled on a fork, was swooping towards his mouth, only for it to be stopped in its tracks, hanging in the air. For my sins, I fought the impulse to smirk myself.

'Bob—yes, let's call him Bob—then bundled his wife's corpse in the bath, where he chopped her up, wrapping up each part in clingfilm and storing them in his freezer. The only problem was that when the parts froze, they expanded to the point he couldn't open the freezer door, at least not without a lot of effort. A lot more effort than it took to murder his spouse in the first place. So, he diligently and arduously lifted each of the body parts back out, defrosted them, and before returning them to the freezer, cut them into more manageable pieces.'

My phone pinged in my back pocket. On inspection it informed me that I was needed elsewhere. 'I need to go, sorry,' I said. 'Stay, enjoy the rest of your meal.'

I left the cash covering my share of the meal on the table. The fork with impaled mushroom was still dangling around Robert-short-for-Bob's mouth, even as I was rising to my feet.

The fork went spiralling, mushroom untouched, back down to his plate. 'Will you arrest me if I don't?' he said.

Oh dear. But I didn't hang around long enough to respond. My date for the evening was put in the same boat as the remaining two courses of Chicken and Pork Morcon (or Potato and Cabbage for the veggie option) and Coconut Pistachio Parfait Snowballs. I wondered—no more than a fleeting flight of fancy, to be honest—if at one time in the future he should find himself in trouble, resulting in him seated in front of me once more, if he would actually come across better than he had tonight. Any warmth we might have shared at the start of the evening was now gone, consigned to a much colder place. To that freezer in Busby.

Which was apt response enough.

9.

Keep Breathing

I arrived as soon as I got the call, or the message, or the ping, or whatever you wanted to call it. I arrived at a scene of carnage, or the aftermath of carnage, where it seemed an impossible task for order to try to impose itself once more. It was a losing battle. You could never hope for order again, or peace or tranquillity. Not after this. A police cordon secured the area, supplemented by squad cars, vans, and I counted two ambulances, supplying all kinds of light, gaining purchase now dusk had descended. Otherwise, the tumult had settled down and the smoke and dust had subsided. I had arrived at Shawlands Drive. I had arrived at a crime scene.

The covering up of the dead.

At more than a crime scene.

I made a beeline to one of the uniformed officers, considered showing him my badge, but delayed that thought as his frame visibly untightened on my approach. He recognised me. It wasn't that important that I didn't recognise him.

'Ma'am,' he said. His frame began to tense up again, unsure of his next response; of how to broach reality as he had only recently come to understand it.

'Bad night,' I said. 'Bad, bad night. It's okay, tell me what you know. What you think.'

'An ambush,' he said. 'Two of our own. Unspeakable. Used a grenade we think. A fucking grenade. Tore one of them apart. As for the other...' He took on a pause which lasted an eternity, but I'd asked the question so I owed him as much to wait it out. 'Ruth Cairns and Ryan Patterson. Two of our own.'

'DI is here already,' he said, seizing the opportunity to move away from the sensational and horrifying, and occupy more solid ground. I had already spotted the DI advancing on one of the ambulances. He had his arm raised in a bid to halt two paramedics who were carrying a stretcher into the back of the vehicle.

My initial emotion was anger. I wanted to walk up to him and scream at him, ask him *why are you here?* I wanted to hit him, force a response, but none of this was acceptable behaviour, not in the present setting. (I suppose not in any setting.) I had to be better than that. I had to swallow it back down again.

The more I wanted to rush at him and knock him off that stupid, imperious perch of his, the more I willed my legs to slow down, to perambulate instead, nothing quicker than a stroll. No interest, show I didn't care.

That said, I reached him in less time than I would have wanted to.

He was looking off into the distance—it couldn't be in response to me suddenly being in the vicinity. His head was elevated and I joined his gaze, directing me to the looming tower that was the Victoria Flats. The queen of all High-Rises, all thirty floors. Such was its dominance, more commonly referred to as simply The Flats.

And I was back on the top of that other building—that other, more modest block of flats. Where I followed his earlier footsteps, without going as far as where the footsteps ended and his descent began, leaving it to my wretched imagination to try to inform me how it must feel. A brutal force, falling at a hundred miles an hour, the instant separation of flesh and blood. He couldn't know this—couldn't know that I was there—gathering himself on a medical bed as he was, in the process of reassembly, in the grip of a miraculous recovery.

As soon as I noticed The Flats, he had already averted his gaze. If he had a newfound revulsion for high buildings, after what he had been through, I wouldn't have blamed him. Meanwhile, the paramedics had come to a halt. Three-quarters of the stretcher was in the ambulance. A white sheet draped over a human being now laid to rest, crystallised in the moment.

The DI was looking at me. I noticed he had a walking stick at his left side, held in his strapped hand.

His ring finger was still missing. (Should I have expected anything different?) The sight of this, all of this, made me feel giddy and now I wanted to laugh, or knock his teeth out, until I realised I had insufficient breath in my lungs, forcing me to wait for someone to instruct me to breathe. To tell me that breathing wasn't wasted on the living. And when someone did eventually say something, it would have to be him, of course.

'DS Spencer, you might want to take a moment,' he said.

***

'DS Spencer, you might want to take a moment,' I said. 'Take a breath.'

I knew she would appear at some point, like a jack-in-the-box or the switching on of a streetlight. I was glad it had turned out to be sooner rather than later, and right now was as opportune a time as any, as I turned to examine the sheet covering the body of PC Ryan Patterson. A light wind circled us, enough to make the fabric of our clothes twitch. Pinched between thumb and forefinger, I lifted the sheet. The material seemed lighter than air. As if, at the first opportunity, it wanted to reveal all of its secrets. As if it wanted a senseless death to have some meaning.

The sheet shifted and in its place was a face that was not a face. There was no skin. There was a sack of blood instead, turned dull red by prolonged exposure to the air; a muscle memory, still retaining much of its shape, the smudged facsimile of what an adult male should look like.

If there was any movement or exhalation of air from those standing around me, I wasn't aware.

'Funny,' I whispered.

'As in funny peculiar,' I said, as way of clarification. Not that I was being particularly insightful or clear. And not that I was willing to explain myself further. I was distracted by a sudden crushing pain around my stump, the remnant of my missing finger on my left hand. The pain was so intense, I considered transferring my walking stick from my left hand to my right.

'You seen this TYPE of thing before?' A voice boomed out all of a sudden. Letters three-dimensional against a 2D backdrop.

'You know you can tell ME. I've seen you, really SEEN you: your body, your insides. You BURST all over me, just like a fucking orange, like a fucking peach. It made a right frigging MESS it did.' The voice wasn't coming from DS Spencer or the paramedics. PC Patterson? If I could be sure of anything, then surely it couldn't be him. The pain in my hand, still there but had dulled some, having flattened out, almost seemed like a welcome distraction.

It occurred to me that I needed to be somewhere else.

'*Ottoman Empire* ANYONE?' the voice said.

'OTTOMAN?'

'ANYONE?'

And I presupposed by anyone, the voice was meaning me.

***

So, it was off to the Bar-L then. Over time, I would inevitably be drawn there, either to signify the end of a case or the beginning, rarely somewhere between. It wasn't too difficult to extricate myself from the crime scene at Shawlands Drive. The harrowing sight of PC Patterson still fresh in our minds, I had a quiet word with DS Spencer.

'I'm tired,' I said.

She nodded.

'I don't suppose you could take over here?'

She nodded some more.

That she agreed to my request so readily both surprised and didn't surprise me. Or to be more exact, since I outranked her and if I wanted to, I could transform a request into an order, that she never sought to push back or complain. We had a past together. We were partners, and I had been found wanting. I was wholly unprofessional. At best I hid things from her, and at worst I obstructed her investigations. I'd been a source of pain for her, a reason the job she loved was taken away from her (thankfully, only on a temporary basis). I suspected that on top of this, and in part because of this, I occupied her thoughts, too many of them, more than she would ever care to admit. Granted, she had every reason to despise and only wish ill of me. I had a lot of ground to make up if I was ever to convince her that she could trust me again. But if that was to happen, it would have to take place at another time. Somewhere else, not Shawlands Drive.

Perhaps I was being unfair here. If I asked her to take over the investigation, why would she say no? You cut each of us in half and, so exposed, when it came down to it, like the middle of a stick of Blackpool rock, it was engraved there: we were all about the case. We were all about the job.

I parked the car at Barlinnie Prison carpark. The passenger seat coughed out my walking stick. I was hungry for the stick. I leaned down on it, various limbs attempting to exit the car in the wrong order. I resembled a contortionist whose performance, having been recorded, was played out at one tenth the normal speed. After a period of inactivity, stuck as I was behind the wheel, random joints seized up and my body stiffened terribly. I tried to tell myself it was all a state of mind. A bloody uncomfortable state of mind, mind you.

A prison guard waited for me at the entrance, tasked with chaperoning me through the maze. To lead me through the eternal noise, the constant closing of steel doors, like the peeling of church bells, in ceaseless ferment, one clashing off the other. There had to be a rationale behind the din. It had to be a thing of faith, or persuasion, that no matter how long the corridors, how soulless or grey, there was the conviction that they must lead somewhere. Perhaps to freedom.

Maybe all the way down to Hell. Serving notice that the Bar-L was a place that existed very much between states. The high road. The low road. The states of mind.

So many old wounds I would very much like to see scab over. There were so many ghosts here, so many I yearned to revisit, if only to keep my distance and draw a fresh line between me and them. There was one wound, though, seeping, bubbling, that I would have to reopen. There was one line that I would have to cross.

'Prisoner is secured,' the guard said, as way of announcement that I had reached my intended destination. 'Just wanted to say from me and the lads,' he quickly added, 'great to see you back. You are a living legend. Fifteen minutes, that do you?'

'Uh, thanks,' I said. This new-found adulation among the police, prison service, more or less anything associated with law and order, was taking a wee while to get used to, but it did have its uses. It had a way of opening doors. 'Make it twenty,' I said.

Nodding, the prison guard opened the door and in I walked.

'Call me SAMURAI,' a voice called out from behind me.

It was the same voice from before; the mysterious booming voice from Shawlands Drive. Now it was in the Bar-L, set on following me in. I contemplated looking back, but at that moment, forward momentum was everything.

I was already in the room, door shut and locked behind me, before I could react further.

'What?' I said, too late. Too late to take back the word. Perhaps I would have cause to revisit it later.

Inside the room, Michael Doherty sat at the end of the table facing me, looking like he didn't have a care in the world. Sandy-haired Michael. Unique in the sense that it had been a couple of years since last we met in this place and he had barely aged. He wore dark orange overalls appropriate to his high security rating. His hands were cuffed in a way that allowed him to rest his arms on the table, but not much else. Even so, he gave me a tiny wave with one hand, veins popping, stretching at the wrist.

'Hello, Michael,' I said.

I placed my walking stick on the table, horizontally, hugging the edge. I took the remaining chair, facing Michael. He had been eighteen years in the Bar-L. Eighteen years and counting. He was institutionalised. In the time he'd spent on this planet, the Bar-L was as much a home to him as any.

'Hello, Inspector,' Michael said, flexing both sets of fingers so they resembled the legs of a badly coordinated spider. 'The screws call you Lazarus now. You're the dude who came back from the dead, and without a moment's hesitation tumbled back into public service. You didn't even take the time to take a shit. It's an honour really. A real honour.'

He looked down at my walking stick. There was an expression of whimsy on his face, if only for a moment or two. After this, he couldn't help but bare his teeth. 'You and your stick,' he said.

'Thank you, Michael,' I said, 'but I only did what anyone would do in my situation.' I adjusted my body position so that part of my arms below the elbow lay flat. My arms were so still, they could have been chained to the table, as much as his was. Equally, there was no life in my seven remaining fingers and two thumbs. 'Your cooperation is appreciated. I'll be sure to put in a good word when they next plonk you in front of the parole board.'

Michael snorted. It was the loudest thing I'd heard today, diminishing the clang of every metal door. A nasal shriek, something worthy of Satao the elephant.

'Up for parole,' he said, 'that's about acknowledging the past. That's about what you do in the future. I did what I did, I'll happily put my hands up.' Fingers did their best to shoot up from shackled wrists, and I noticed for what seemed like the first time, but surely it couldn't be, how small his hands were, relative to the rest of him. 'But I can't account for what I do in the future. I'll be a good boy. A solid civilian. Promise I won't touch what I'm not entitled to. But I can't say that. I can't control the future. No one can.'

'I can't find fault with your logic,' I said. 'As for me, I'm mainly interested in the past, maybe a smattering of the present. Of course, anything of substance that comes out of this little conversation is just between you and me. You bunked with him for a while. I want to talk about *Horse Peter*.'

'It'll cost you.'

'I promise to try to meet your price.'

'You can do better than that.'

'I can only promise to try, like you say...'

'I can't control the future.' He finished my sentence, and grinned. He knew what I was getting at. I was getting at what he was getting at.

'Horse Peter...' he said. There was a glint in one eye, and then the next. There was an echoey quality to his voice. 'Horse Peter...'

'With a name like that,' he said, 'everyone thought he was some big-time drug dealer, but the thing is, he had a thing about horses. What else—snort—is there to know?'

'Specifically?' I wasn't averse to answering questions, even if the job description was all about asking them. 'He broke into the police stables in Tannoch, oh, fifteen, sixteen years ago and fed one of the horses ketamine, crushed in with sugar cubes. The horse was in a state of ketamine-induced anaesthesia when he broke its neck then proceeded to skin its face off with a hunting knife.' The memory was strong, recent, indecent, vivid, restored from a dream. If I closed my eyes, it pulsated, all the colours embroidering the back of my eyelids, like moving pictures from a projector. A dream of Tannoch. 'You may know this, Michael, but it was me from all those years ago who discovered the horse.'

Blood still dripping from its muzzle. Taking its own time.

'Ka-ching,' he said, his eyes dancing, revelling in the projected nostalgia of it all. 'You think they put you in Bar-L for killing horses?'

'Michael, you know they don't.'

'Four days later,' I continued, 'Peter boards the end carriage of a Glasgow underground train wearing a horse head mask and armed with said knife. One frenzied attack later and we have two passengers dead, several more seriously wounded. That, Michael, is what they put you in Barlinnie for.'

'Like I said—snort—he had a thing about horses.' Michael's eyes had lost much of their previous sheen. 'I shared a cell with him for a few weeks. Horse Peter didn't say much. He borrowed the odd library book. I suppose he did open up to me, maybe, once or twice. You remember everything in here like it was yesterday. His horse mask was made of rubber, something he'd bought in a toy shop, but had bits of horse's face sewed on. As in real horse. Skinned horse. Sliced and diced horse. He had a flair for the taxidermy, I guess. You get a lot of that in here.'

'He saw the mask as a mixture of symbolism and convenience, I don't know, words don't make sense in the Bar-L, they're not designed to. Who can separate the half-truths from the all-out fucking lies? Not the pricks with words coming out of their mouths. Peter might have gone back further, four days you say, and told me about the time he broke into the Tannoch stables and flayed that horse of his. Think about it, that night anything could have gone wrong. He could have been caught red-handed at any time. But he wasn't. And knowing Horse Peter he would have put it down to some destiny bollocks.'

Michael laughed, keen to share a joke all of a sudden, 'Red-handed, get it? Literally, red fucking hands!'

I put my hands up, mouth forming an upturn that could barely qualify as a quarter-smile. I wasn't here to humour him. He certainly wasn't here to humour me. 'I get it, Michael,' I said.

'No need to bust a gut or anything, Inspector,' he said, indignant, the nascent formation of a growl embedded in his throat.

I couldn't say at which point it started, but he had become agitated. Borderline wild. I was unsure which way he would go. Would he embrace the full wolfman or calm back down again? But Michael was a big boy and if I had caused offence, however inadvertently, he was the one who needed to come to terms with it.

'He's all FRONT, fucking bellend, has nothing in his locker. Give him a minute, he'll FOLD like a fucking puppy.'

There it was again, coming out of nowhere, but I ignored the voice this time. I was slightly reassured by the fact Michael was acting like he hadn't heard a thing. But even so, it was undeniable, there was something to it. There was something to that voice.

Michael reverted to his glacier state of before. 'By telling me this,' he said, 'Horse Peter might have been reaching out to me. Human being to human being.

Fucked up human being to fucked up human being. But my head was too full to bursting as it was. I still had some of my face back then—my fresh face—and I had enough chicanery to deal with in the Bar-L already without taking on any more.'

'I appreciate it was a long time ago,' I interjected. 'There was a fight inside your cell. Peter lost over a litre of blood. He required stitches in his neck and tongue.'

'It is what it is,' Michael said, his voice trailing off, culminating in silence. As much silence as the cauldron of noise which enveloped our little room would allow.

I was in danger of losing him. Michael knew this as much as I did. And I wasn't ready to take my leave of him just yet. He had more to tell, I could feel it in my water. There would be a price to pay, though.

I leaned forward, ready to hear it.

'But Detective,' he said, 'taking trips down memory lane is very well, but that's all I've got in this place. Between these walls, memories, something to block out the shouting and screaming. The begging. The smell of nonces pissing themselves asleep. And me, I try not to think about women, not once. Always happy to cooperate with the law, and I'm not one of those nutcases who hates the filth no matter what. The ones who'd beat you to a pulp at the sight of you. Would fuck you up any which way. You know that. I've helped before. But fair is fair, you want something from me, you have to give something back—'

'You have to give something up of him.'

You could have knocked me down with a feather, but that wouldn't have prevented me from knowing what he was getting at—*who* he was getting at. I knew what he wanted. He wanted the *other* me. They all wanted a piece of him. He had become elevated somehow among the criminal underworld, some kind of bogeyman, some kind of cult hero in equal measure. It was bewildering. It would make your eyes water, if you weren't prone to biting your bottom lip, which you'd found stopped this from happening.

'I'm not that man anymore, Michael,' I said. 'That part of me is gone. It left me when they scraped me up piece by piece off the ground and put me in a hospital bed.'

Michael had a look of alarm on his face, on the verge of bursting into tears. It was a juggling act on my part, always, judging how far to push, then pull, before I lost him forever.

'Show him your STUMP,' the voice called out. It was no use, and I had long given up trying to locate where the voice was coming from. There was only me and Michael in the room, and currently we weren't raising a squeak between us.

Was it my old self coming back to haunt me? No, I'd suffered too much, worked too hard, sacrificed too much for this to be even a remote possibility. For the first time I was in control of things. I was clean. My hands were clean.

All the while, the tape around my left hand seemed to tighten. It had to be a trick of the mind, but real or imagined, the discomfort was palpable. I examined my bandaged hand and searched for a fold, a crease, something I could bother, threads I could pull. In my desperation, I tore a small strip from the tape, teasing it clear. Then, between two fingers, I took hold of the next, wider and longer strip, generating one circular motion after another, reducing the incumbent mass. Ever more, this revealed spoiled skin having turned purple, having been deprived of air, of light, of blood supply. The tape shrunk until reduced to the last bastion of strapping, situated directly around the wound of my severed finger. The finger that was snipped off with secateurs by a priest turned madman called Connor with a man-eating dog for a pet; the dog now dead, the priest now incarcerated. For all I knew, he could be imprisoned in the cell right next to the room I currently occupied.

There was no more picking of threads to be done, or tearing off of strips. I dug my fully functioning fingers from my right hand into what was left of the tape, ripping it off. A line of lumpy white discharge gushed forth, on the same course as the receding tape, before breaking off.

I bared my teeth, with no end to the maddening, aching discomfort in sight. I lifted my fully exposed left hand for Michael to see. All that remained of my finger showed clear signs of infection, the wraparound skin a dark green, the stump infiltrated by a soapy white pus.

'This,' I said, rotating my wrist, discharge running

down front and back of my hand, 'is all I have to remember him by.'

'We're all FRIENDS together...'

'We're all friends together,' I said, 'tell me Michael, what else is there to know? He tried to make a connection with you, I get that, but in his time in the Bar-L was there anyone else you'd say Peter was close to?'

Michael stared at the stump like it was some holy relic. Something to gaze upon with something like awe. He closed his eyes, then opened them, then looked up, reverential, making a show of searching the memory banks.

'There was one,' Michael said. 'A right weirdo.' He blew through his lips continuously, making a helicopter sound. 'Brrrrpp.' His eyes shifted from side to side. 'You could say he got close. But to be fair, he was a real networker that one. Was nothing he wouldn't do to get in your good books, if you follow? You could do anything to him, and he took it. After the event, it hardly seemed to matter to him anymore. But the thing is, how can I put it, he seemed comfortable with Horse Peter, and Horse Peter seemed comfortable with him. Near the end, Horse Peter was considered a model prisoner. Didn't put a foot wrong. No plans to let him out anytime soon, but no longer high security. Still, Horse Peter gave nothing away, but with this one, he'd be whispering in his ear. No pillow biting, just to be sure—snort—just the development of a strong bond. We're all rats in here. Crawling over each other, leaving our mark. Yeah, this one, he was close to Horse Peter. He was called Peter as well. Which is funny, yeah? As in funny fucking hilarious?'

It must have been a trick of the light, but for a second, I could have sworn that Michael was leaning back and crossing his arms, which of course, his shackles binding him to this earth and to this table, was impossible. What wasn't impossible were the words coming out of his mouth.

'So, I think now,' he said, 'now it's your turn.'

'OK...'

I lowered my left hand until it was almost resting on the table and then as reflex, I brought it back up again. I stared intensely at the infected, drooling stub.

'OK...'

I reached out with my hand—my *other* hand—fingers and thumb twitching and curled, curled and twitching. Was it my hand? I'd forgotten as much, so I had to remind myself. It was so close to me, enough to be unbearable. I was aware that, somewhere, a light was about to go out. A pulse, a beat, a seizure, a shifting of the natural order.

'OK...'

I grabbed the stump and squeezed hard. The flaps of skin gave way easily. My hand filled with sticky juice.

I could control this.

I could go through the motions. I could create a poor representation. A crude facsimile of the man I once was. I didn't know if it would work but was obligated to try; to give Michael a glimpse. A fair exchange for agreeing to talk with me. Because I'm good like that.

The pain flowed through me, piercing me in places far from the neutered roots of my severed finger. It was as if my brain, so fearful yet so familiar with pain, sought to parcel and redistribute it throughout my body. I had known so much pain. It belittled me, persecuted me; a fuse was lit, blazing a trail through my skull. And still I kept squeezing, unearthing a memory that I could never claim to call my own, but a memory nonetheless.

'There is a place I would sometimes go...' I said/he said.

'There is a place I would sometimes go. A dilapidated, disused building located in the East End. You could tell this by the fact that the brownstone was crumbling from the outside of the building. You only had to look at it funny for the bricks to erode some more. Derelict, windows boarded up, "Keep Out" signs hanging by a single rusted screw. But not quite abandoned. Nature abhors a vacuum. It's a cliché, but it's true. I'd walk inside, keeping what I touched of the interior to a minimum, careful too of where I put my feet. There was a room on the ground floor, in the belly of the building, where the floorboards were still relatively intact. No furniture: all there was for sitting on were two beanbags, one nearer the door, which was unoccupied, the other against the wall on the other side of the room. Carefully, I'd lift my feet and take the one available beanbag. Made myself as comfortable as I could in such a hell-forsaken shithole. A teenager, male from what I could ascertain and for all I cared, would sit on the other beanbag. His skin all kinds of patterns and colours. His arms and torso exposed, covered in all sizes of scars and scabs. I'd go there and watch the boy shoot up. We both knew the drill, both abided by the unspoken rule; I was strictly a spectator. I could not intervene in any shape or form—and I would not intervene. I was there for the ritual, a movement, the chaotic flurry of limbs as he searched for a vein he could use, or one he could risk using again.'

At this point in the telling of the story, I wanted to break into a smile, but I had to check myself and fight it all back down again. I couldn't allow myself to enjoy the performance. To revel in it. That would be too undignified. Too unprofessional. I had to exile such desires to an empty space inside of me. 'Like I said, there is a place I would sometimes go. The mistake was that by coming back, I'd make myself vulnerable. My bad. That latest time, some ned looking to curry favour with the criminal fraternity came at me through the door. He rushed me with a baseball bat. But he was unprepared, hopeless, he didn't lift his feet. He tripped on the tripwire located at the door. I was already up, reflexes of a panther on full display, isn't that how the legend goes, and I was ready for him. I had already positioned my knee, so he cracked his nose off it as he fell.'

'He lay on his back, blood spurting out his nose like

it was the Doulton Fountain. I waited for the blood to subside. This took two, maybe three minutes. The ned began to moan, so I stepped on his chest and kept my foot there until he stopped. Then I sat myself back down and waited for the boy on the other beanbag to resume his business. I sat and watched as he slowly, laboriously, silently, curled the bare filthy brown sole of his foot towards the needle in his shaking hand.'

I closed then opened my eyes to confirm I was still in the Bar-L. I shook my head. I didn't believe a word I'd just said, but that wasn't the point. Someone did.

'Thank you, thank you,' Michael said. His face was beaming. Even if he'd wanted to, he could not hide his delight. The criminal fraternity's fear and worship in equal measure of my former alter ego was on record. In this respect I pitied Michael. In so many ways I wished things were so different.

I had already grabbed my walking stick from the table. I was already in the process of standing to leave.

'A pinch of snuff here, the first use of a Kinder Egg there. I'll be dining out on this for weeks,' he said.

'I'm not that man anymore,' I said.

These were my parting words, as it happened. I moved away from the pain at the table, only to find that it had followed me to the door. There, I held my walking stick between my legs, which caused both knees to stick out at a pronounced angle. This allowed me to use my right hand to hold the wrist of my violated, diseased left hand. Leaving me with my forehead, which I used to knock on the metal door, confirmation to any interested parties of my desire to leave. The metal was cold to the brow.

'Then who am I in the room with?' Michael asked from behind me, his words in delirious pursuit.

But they were only words.

10.

Date No. 2

I was high up. So high I could feel the world shift under my feet. No sign of life, at least directly below me. No movement or stamping or water running out of a tap. No sweat and no tears.

I had done a bad thing. I had been a fraudster, a prostitute, an addict, a common thief, and now I was a murderer. The man from Army & Navy Surplus had taken a minute to show me how to prime a grenade, but when it came to it, it had come naturally. The terrible cruelty of it; the starkness of it; the eclipsing of one's moral compass; I looked forward to that day when the ramifications of what I did—the horror—would lessen in time. Five hundred years in the future, what would it matter who lived now and how they died? We'd all be gone by then, along with those who would claim to have remembered us.

I needed to be inhumane. I needed to embrace the

concept to the point of liking the sound of it, how the letters rolled off the tongue.

There was no power in my room, no means of generating heat and light, but I am a hardy creature. I desire and want for very little. It was frustrating to think that if everyone followed my lead, lived at the very limit of subsistence, of endurance, how less a strain this would place on the fragile ecosystem which surrounds us. A planet presently on its knees could replenish scarce resources, step back from the brink of extinction, and turn things around. We could all be alive to see it.

We could all be truly alive. So much. If only.

I couldn't think about these things for too long. Snakes were crawling in my head. My scalp was red raw. There was pressure, too much pressure, and no prospect of escape from it.

Situated at both ends of the flat, the only windows were boarded up. There were gaps in the wooden slats, sufficient to peer out of and allow in some sunlight. Sometimes, when I wanted to have a better view, I would prise out the nails and remove some boards, but it wouldn't be long before I'd hammer them back on again. There was a single mattress on the floor. A Bag for Life sat on top of the mattress. There was no running water and the toilet no longer flushed, but there were enough accessible flats around me for this not to be a problem so far. I lived frugally, sparingly. A typical meal would be a banana and some dried bread. I could make a tin of tomato soup last for days.

The time had come, if only for a short while, to dispense with my trusty balaclava. I had tried, I always do, but I couldn't put the moment off any longer. With both hands I began to peel off my second skin. As the balaclava wool rolled up my face, a sense of both grief and panic took over my mind, infiltrated my guts. Things were going to get worse before they could possibly get any better. I now looked down and saw I was holding the balaclava in my hand. I let it go, allowing it to fall to the ground. I couldn't breathe. I was terribly exposed.

I put my hand in the Bag for Life and took out a pig's mask, three layers, life-like, and washable. In addition, there were strips of skin sewn on. Real skin. Human skin.

Using a borax solution, I'd done my best to preserve as much of the epidermis as possible. What skin I could save, and hadn't stitched on to the mask, I stored in a couple of used jam jars.

I held the neck of the pig mask over the crown of my head and I pulled it down. The material kissed my face several times as it lowered around my face. It fitted like a mask should do. It fitted like a glove.

I opened my mouth, my jaw clicking as I did so. I breathed in the air greedily while sucking in the latex, so it was part of me. Emboldened by sprinkles of human flesh, elevated by suffering and pain, totemic, it was hidden but in full view. Another's spirit so incarcerated in the layers. This was no ordinary mask, it was something more. A second skin. I thought of

Horse Peter and for the first time I thought I could at least put forward the case that I was no longer in his shadow. I didn't have to be in awe of him, not anymore. If I chose not to be. I no longer needed to imagine what it was like to be in the carriage of an underground train. A vision, a ghost, a collection of shade and light, a sharpened blur. The definition of calm one moment, in a state of frenzy the next, lashing out, once balletic, now imprecise, killing things, scarring things, mastering extinction.

Unlike anyone else in this world, I can remember everything about him. The shape of his neck, his hands, his teeth. The sound of his voice, such a distant voice, never raised. Often, he would only whisper.

Projected to other places. He would whisper in my ear and we would no longer be in the Bar-L. No longer trapped inside so many walls. We would be somewhere else. Riding the giant sandworms of Arrakis. We'd be in a forest where the light would catch the leaves, and sometimes we'd be running to something, other times running from something. Steam trains, garden parties, the rings of Saturn, a foetus growing inside a mother's tummy, a city of skyscrapers. He would speak in such hushed tones, and he would say, '*There is one journey I cannot join you on. The one where you find your own face. Just like I did.*'

And it struck me—and it would keep on striking me—out of sight, out of mind over so many years, Horse Peter by rights should no longer exist. But I had to preserve his memory somehow, and by doing so justify my own existence, my every action, no matter how questionable. That was the point of me, to keep Horse Peter alive.

I was rejuvenated. I was ready to embrace life and cast all my anxieties aside and take on the world. I was for the world and I was squealing like a pig. And all it took was a rubber mask.

***

I was down in the catacombs. It was dark down here, a nice kind of dark. I could hear the clink of glass on glass as I walked past bar staff. I liked the sound of it, finding it oddly comforting. Trevor had arrived a few steps before me, allowing him to nab the seat at our table with its back against the wall, which kind of irked me.

He was up on his feet when he saw me, and he waited until I took my seat before he sat back down. It would have been unreasonable to expect him to offer to swap seats. If he did, it would make the situation awkward, or more awkward than it already was, although he wasn't to know any of that, as I kept my irritation to myself. So, I took the seat facing him, my back to the rest of the pub, and things immediately felt flat as a result. Oh, that and the fact when he was standing I noticed he hadn't done up his fly.

'Trevor? I'm Julie,' I said.

'The police detective,' he said, 'you come here often?'

'Pardon?' I said, my eyes beginning to water.

'This place,' he said, 'the Bier Hall. We're in the basement, underground. It's hard to get a signal.'

I willed with all my might for Trevor not to take out his phone, but even before I'd fully formulated the thought, he'd pulled it out of his pocket. At least as a by-product of this, he'd now noticed the fly situation.

'Sometimes I prefer it that way,' I said. 'Not having a signal. In my line of work, you know, it's difficult to get away.'

He bobbled on his seat and adjusted his bottom half in the process of *discretely* pulling up his zip. None of this was helped by a quiet grunt which escaped his lips as he did so. There was no chance in hell I wanted his chair now.

His composure fully restored, if not his dignity, he said, 'You're used to basements in your line of work I suspect.'

There was an itch just above my right knee that I refused to scratch. I didn't want to be the type who made an immediate decision when I'd only just laid eyes on a first date, but not wanting to be that type of person didn't always mean you weren't, in fact, that type of person.

When I first saw Trevor, I thought he was in his 30s. Now, I thought he was in his 40s.

'All kinds,' he said.

'Pardon?'

'They sell all kinds of beers down here,' he said. 'You like Japanese beers?'

'Do they get you drunk?'

I realised at that point that I liked asking questions. I'd realised this many times previously, it was part of the job description, but to *like* asking them, to enjoy it, that kind of realisation never failed to surprise me. What's more I liked answering questions with a question. I couldn't imagine a job or a life that didn't involve the constant asking of questions. I feared that this dating game might go on forever, one man after another. I'd collect enough of them to fill the Albert Hall, always, never failing to ask questions. Stuck in the rut of forever avoiding giving answers of my own.

'Have you ever been to Japan?' I said.

The look on his face conveyed utter confusion. He was seconds away from his head spinning and detaching from his shoulders. I sat like I was made of stone and I couldn't see his problem. It seemed like a reasonably simple enough question to me.

'I'm from Elderslie,' he said.

One of the bar staff appeared ready to take our order.

'Sapporo,' he said.

'Nothing for me,' I said.

Another look, this one the polar opposite to the one before. This time he knew exactly what I was getting at. 'Before you go, can I kiss you?' he said.

Did he deserve a kiss? Why so inattentive, why so dismissive? To be blunt, he was a terrible listener. Perhaps that could be a useful trait. I'd have someone to talk to; to say anything I liked, all the dark, brooding thoughts that occurred to me, and with his cloth ears he'd do little more than nod and come out of it relatively unscathed. Relationships could be built on a lot less.

I wasn't there yet, so I took a breath. One final attempt to get his attention. 'There was an investigation in Elderslie,' I said. 'An elderly gentleman went missing. He was there one minute and then he was gone, or so it seemed. Even though we suspected foul play, we couldn't find a body. Couldn't find any evidence that a crime had been committed. We were stumped. I visited my mum that night and she had seen an advert on the TV for a vacuum cleaner, a Dyson I think, one specially made for hoovering up pet hair. And the way she described it to me, such a diminutive appliance but what suction power, it was like magic was played out in front of her eyes. You see she remembered, as way of contrast, the old style hoover, with those big disposable bags and the noise they made like a wild animal with a bellyache was trapped inside. And how back then it was near impossible to pick up cat hairs, especially those hairs that got entangled in the fibres of the carpet. And now, something like a decade on, with all that wondrous suction, the modern hoover by comparison is some kind of electrical floor and upholstery Norse God. Removing all traces. Making like your pet never existed.'

'Next morning,' I continued, 'I'm back in Elderslie in order to seize the elderly gentleman's cordless vacuum and send it over to forensics. Someone in a white coat finds in the hoover bin, among the usual assorted fluff, dust, dirt and hair, some molar teeth. After a more detailed search of the house, a body was discovered, which leads to an arrest, which leads to a successful conviction.'

Trevor listened on patiently, leaning forward, hands spread flat on the table, thumbs forming the two adjacent lines of a triangle. He smiled at me, and I found myself smiling back. But it wasn't a smile of approval.

'Don't call me, I'll call you?' he said.

'That's the idea,' I said. I got out my own phone, before shaking it in his general direction. 'But, you know, reception.'

I got to my feet.

As did he, while continuing to lean towards me over the table. I didn't flinch. I let him kiss me on the cheek. Right there and then, I found myself on the verge of liking him, but not enough for me to go into reverse.

'Nice,' he said, as an opened bottle of Sapporo was delivered to the table.

'Nice,' I said, and left him to sit back down and enjoy his drink. I still had the phone in my hand as I climbed the stairs and braved the stinging air.

Memorable for all the wrong reasons, I'd forgotten about the date already. It was a diversion, an unexpectedly noteworthy one in places, but it couldn't go on forever. It wasn't my intention to fully escape from reality. Maybe I would have been better served going home instead and trying to get some sleep.

It began to rain. And the rain provided an excuse not to do it. We hadn't spoken since the events of yesterday at Shawlands Drive when he'd asked me to take over. When he'd made a quick exit, walking stick in hand.

Which I did. I took over from the DI and did the best I could. Two of our own dead. I had to take out the emotion and conduct the investigation methodically, properly, professionally, and WPC Ruth Cairns and PC Ryan Patterson, I did right by them. And now, twenty-four hours on, I wasn't sure if I was still on the case. If I should be reporting to him. No one had told me otherwise and everything was up in the air, and all today I hadn't been able to get through to anyone.

Fudge it, I decided I would call him now. Not that he would answer anyway. It was raining. Call him and be done with it.

***

My flat was still alien to me. The rooms, the kitchen, the landing. I would find myself staring at an unfamiliar wall, then waking from my reverie with a start, experiencing a sensation along the lines of standing in the middle of a road facing oncoming traffic. I wondered momentarily why I wasn't in my hospital bed, and then I came to my senses and grasped the fact that my finger hurt.

Or what was left of my finger. I stumbled into my unfamiliar bathroom where I removed the dressing the prison doctor had applied after my interview in the

Bar-L with Michael Doherty. My stump was inflamed, a number of purples, blacks and blues; excruciating to the touch. Even the thought of touch, the sensation of it, was too much to bear.

I stood over the sink in front of the bathroom mirror. I looked at my reflection and used this to create distance from me and my body. I was wearing a plain white t-shirt, which was clean; the source of no confusion at all. I ushered in some activity and held in my good hand, which hovered over my bad hand, a tube of antibiotic cream.

I squeezed. Cool white gloss solution ejaculated onto pulped tissue. I could feel every tiny, jagged molecule, screaming blue murder at me. 'Nnngg...' A noise escaped my mouth, the reflection in the bathroom mirror in front of me confirming its source. '...Sugar,' I said.

'PUSSY!' Another noise, but this one was different. I could see with my own eyes that this voice did not come from me, or my reflection.

Then, another sound, an angry buzzing. My phone was the source, lying on the shelf above the sink. The vibrations of the phone caused it to shake, jump. If left to its own devices, it would surely fall in. Fall in the wet sink. What was I to do? I wasn't myself, but then again when had I last been anything but? At least I could make the shaking stop—

I swiped the screen. In the melee, I'd turned on the speaker. 'Hullo,' I said.

'DI.'

'DS Spencer, it's good to hear from you.'

'I wasn't sure if I should call.'

'No, I need to apologise for abandoning you. For not being in touch.'

'No apology needed, DI, but I thought I should give you my report. None of the neighbours on Shawlands Drive reported anything. This despite previous to the attack, a ground flat door being kicked open. There was a female screaming. The female in question, a Fiona Murray, traumatised of course, but other than this largely unharmed. She interacted with the killer. She's given us a description, told us about the ski mask. He handed her a note, apparently. In terms of other witnesses, the passer-by who made the call—didn't give her name but mentioned she was walking her dog—hasn't come forward either.'

I concentrated on every word. I valued everything DS Spencer had to say. I knew she disliked me, didn't trust me, and I didn't blame her for any of this. Anything she considered important to divulge, to give up, was always worth listening to. She was worth keeping close. It was important to me to be in touch. For her to have a reason to get in touch. Not that I'd normally pick up the phone to her.

'We're on our own,' I said.

'We're on our own,' she repeated back, but there was scant evidence of life in her voice. She sounded tired. She sounded beyond tired.

'Thanks for the update, DS Spencer. You should get some rest.'

'See you tomorrow.'

'Tomorrow?'

'The funeral, it's tomorrow.'

'Ah, of course,' I said, 'tomorrow.'

She ended the call. I lowered my hand and stared at the screen for several seconds until it went dark.

'Fucking PUSSY!' the voice went.

'Okay,' I said to no one in particular. 'We need to talk.'

11.

A Darker Blue

In the course of an investigation, I had done it all. Following leads, checking out suspicious activity, moving from one room to another, walking from the light into the darkness. I'd made a career out of it. The light could be dazzling, so much so I'd need to squint my eyes to minimise the glare, to hold my hand up as a makeshift shield, to fill the room with icy breath. And the dark, it was inescapable. You could wear it like a cloak, ignoring the truth that it wore *you* like a cloak, how it turned your senses and footing against you. You couldn't block that sort of thing out. Accompanying it, a sense of foreboding that made you think twice about reaching out and fumbling for the light. How it changed you, the transition from dark to light, not knowing what lay in wait for you. A drug den, an explosion of violence, an Aladdin's cave, a room populated by twisted forms of life. The anticipation could warp you. The reality could change your whole personality.

No, I couldn't block it out, the voice inside my head. I had to face it instead, head on, so to speak. Or at least that was the idea. I stood facing a heavy wooden door. The door had a keyhole and I thought about crouching down to peer through, if only to ascertain whether the door was locked from the other side. That's when I thought, *what was the point?* The door was part of my imagination. Any notion of there being a key and a locked door was purely in passing. If it wasn't immediately obvious to me where the key was, its location had to be lurking somewhere inside my head. There was a voice attached to the key. A voice that had already announced itself. A voice I think, at a push, I recognised but didn't want to recognise, not while it still hid in the shadows like a potty-mouthed cowardly lion. Not when my mindscape could happily conjure up a yellow brick road to skip and gesticulate on and get the cuffs out when faced with unacceptable levels of resistance. It was my dream. It would reveal its true nature soon enough. It was a case of just sitting tight and waiting.

'Hullo, is there anyone out there?' I'd decided it wouldn't do any harm to try and instigate proceedings. To hurry things along.

At this, the door swung open. There was something missing from the door's movement, which leant it a lack of authenticity. There was no sound.

'SQUEAK,' a voice called from inside the room.

Some people will deny anything including the truth, even and maybe especially, when it's staring you in the face. I wasn't one of those people. I walked in and found myself face to face with Bryce Coleman.

'You're dead,' I said.

'You KILLED me,' he said.

'Well, I wouldn't say that was...'

Bryce Coleman held up a hand, shot up from the wrist, straight, uncompromising, unambiguous. He was looking remarkably well, all things considered. He wore a white shirt with a tie, hanging loose around the neck. The tie was a dark blue.

We were in a windowless room with brick walls. Taking centre stage was a large wooden table with no chairs. On top of the table was a large whisky decanter with two glasses. It may have been my mind, but this was Bryce Coleman's domain.

'You FELL on me from a fucking great height,' he said. 'You were a MISSILE. I NEVER stood a chance. Not a BLOODY chance.'

'It wasn't my...'

He shook his head and blew air out of his mouth. He lifted the decanter, filling up the two glasses with a clear brown liquid.

'We are WHERE we are. Let bygones be BYGONES. Turn the other ARSE cheek. SEE, off the tip of my tongue I can roll out one useless inane cliché after another. Just like the next man, BETTER than the next man. Wouldn't want to be the NEXT man. I just want to talk, parlay, CHEW the fat. Maybe I scratch your back, you CAN scratch mine with a loofah; a shitty stick; a plank of wood.'

'I'm not following...'

He thrust a glass of whisky in my hand. He did so with such force the liquid leapt out of the glass, then splashed down again with an extended plop. He produced an ice cube from his other hand, flicking it with his thumb in the direction of my glass. The ice cube made a second plop as it made its target.

He looked down at both of his hands. 'My hands are FREEZING,' he said. 'I can't feel my HEART inside my chest. When I bang my head against a wall, I DON'T feel a thing. I NEED something to keep me occupied, a project to keep me sane.'

'I don't know what you...'

'You NEVER came to my funeral.' He started tying his tie, each end flapping this way and the other. On closer inspection, the tie was now as dark a blue as it was possible to be. Any darker and it would be something else. 'I was Roy Lichtenstein's favourite SON and you never came. I was a BIG name. I had RESPECT. I had FEAR. Scumbags, the lowest of the low, would CUT their mother's throat just to get noticed by me.'

'I don't believe you're...'

He took a cigar out of his sleeve and held it above his eyeline in order to gaze up at it before dropping it in his mouth. The cigar expanded comically like it was a cigar from a cartoon. He swallowed it in one gulp like *he* was a cartoon.

I watched the cigar's cylindrical shape stick out and seesaw down his cartoon throat.

'What makes you SAY that?' he said. 'Who gave you the RIGHT?'

I leaned back. I recoiled. I could feel the air whipping around my ears. The room was moving; its contours adjusting around and lurching past me. A pratfall, legs in the air, but my back didn't hit the floor. Instead, I fell out the door, which was slammed shut after me.

I opened my eyes.

I opened my eyes with the knowledge that former crime boss Bryce Coleman, now deceased, had set up camp inside my head. Why he was there, I did not know. I could think about it, but this would scramble my brain, which was already scrambled enough.

I was back in the real world. Although if such a world included me, an identifiable part of it, how could it be trusted? How real could it be?

I badly wanted to gather up some momentum. I was at my most vulnerable, mentally as well as physically, when standing still.

I dressed my hand, and then I dressed the rest of me. I dressed for the occasion where the formality of a uniform, while preferable, was not compulsory, which was just as well. Before the accident, a good few months ago, I'd taken my uniform to a drycleaner, but I hadn't had the chance to pick it up since returning. I was glad the decision was made for me. The uniform made me feel like an imposter, so instead I wore a black suit, a plain cream double cuff shirt, and a dark blue tie. I had turned my flat upside down that morning but could not find a black one. I had a vague memory of one being somewhere, tucked in a safe place. Too safe a place as it turned out. Clothes and accessories, medals and knickknacks were strewn everywhere until the flat resembled a crime scene, a building site. And the black tie was still nowhere to be found.

I felt the frustration build up inside me. Maybe I should ask around, I thought. Maybe someone will have a spare tie tucked away in the glove compartment of their car. But that would entail taking the initiative and picking up the phone and contacting another soul, but I was too far gone for that, such were the state of my nerves. I was a pool of sweat. The thought of any kind of human interaction terrified me. I know such a revelation would surprise some. I wasn't at all averse *in* the company of people. It was only the prospect of such that frightened me. The prospect of letting everyone down.

I gulped down, wondering how long I'd need to wait until the saliva stopped flooding my mouth. I could feel the mania climbing up my back like a hand pretending it was a spider. I took deep breaths. I rolled my neck until I could hear the bone click out and then into place. I counted my fingers, kept counting them, until I didn't feel that way anymore.

1-2-3-4-5-6-7-8-9...

1-2-3-4-5-6-7-8-9...

I had a mug of sweet tea (two-and-a-half heaped

tablespoons of sugar). I promised my overworked brain that, over the time it would take to drink my tea, I would call a ceasefire on thinking. For a smidgen over three minutes, I was a blank page, the odd slurp besides.

There was a knock on the door. I wasn't fully dressed and my hair badly needed a comb. I was a little on the shambolic side to be honest, but aesthetics apart I had no reason not to answer. Having finished my cup of tea, I found it within me to reset. Walking a tightrope, walking in a straight line as if part of a sobriety test, then a stumble, a healing then relapse. I was sometimes in need of a walking stick, to bend and crook, to not only take my bodyweight but all my neuroses as well. And then there were other times when I could walk unaided. The stick—the wrong end of the stick or the right end—I found I could deal with the pain without it.

No reason not to open the door. No reason not to reveal, standing on the other side, the Chief Superintendent. He clocked the fact that, past my ramshackle appearance, I wasn't wearing my uniform, but let this pass without comment, at least verbally. His eyes shifted from one side to the other like an old cash register. The Super stood tall, resplendent in his uniform. The buttons on his jacket weren't only polished, they dazzled.

'Sir,' I said. I spent a few moments considering whether I should salute, then decided against it, a moot point by then as I had taken too long to decide one way or the other. I needed to work on my game. Get up to speed.

'Fisher,' he said.

As the Super said the words, he looked over my shoulder. He gave out a little cough as he peered into the mess which constituted the innards of my flat. No sooner had he his fill of this, his gaze centred on the very dark but ultimately blue tie looped around my neck.

'Trouble finding a black tie, is it?' he said. 'I have a squad car waiting downstairs. I'm sure there's a spare in the glove compartment.' He lay a hand on the shoulder he had been staring past only moments before. 'You've got five minutes, go finish getting changed. There's something I want to talk to you about on the drive over.'

'Sir.' I turned 180 degrees.

'Another thing,' he said.

'Sir?' I turned another 180 degrees.

'Don't you need your walking stick?'

'Not today, Sir.'

Super nearly mouthed a word, a name, but stopped himself. The name of the man brought to life by Jesus as related by the Gospel According to John.

'Not today, Sir,' he said instead. On balance, easier for him to repeat my words from earlier.

12.

The Funeral of Ruth Cairns

I was present at the funeral of Ruth Cairns. A black sea of uniformed officers wound its steady way in front of me, carrying a lake of red poppies. There must have been three hundred bowed heads, although I'd lost count well before that. Behind the crowd stood several trees, spaced apart, unflinching giants, the extent of their roots naked to the eye. Overhead, a flock of birds swayed while rigidly sticking to a grid system of their own choosing, an allotment of sky. And one God. I knew Ruth Cairns was a practising Catholic, so He owed her that much to be present as well.

I was standing on an incline, the start of a hill, and the ground beneath my feet was a little soft. Droplets had formed on the green-yellow grass. A fly buzzed past, not outstaying its welcome. We were all standing in a wind trap. I had never known a graveyard to be anything other.

My throat was dry. My mouth tasted of chalk. And I thought of my mum. I couldn't help it. I thought of all the conversations I wish we could still have had. A longing to touch her face one more time and whisper into her ear and tell her that I loved her and missed her. I missed her smile, even though it was years since I'd last seen it. The last few years were hard on her, but to breathe the same air as her, to cry the same tears as her... I could afford myself at least this much in these surroundings, the capacity to be merciful and kind. I could think of Mum and forgive myself.

And there he was. Lord Muck. The Second Coming. Lazarus. Call-me-Brian. The flow of the crowd shifted around him like the parting of the Red Sea. Slipping from one mourner to another, he shook every hand that stretched out to him.

I was afraid the intensity I felt, endured even, after my mum's passing was beginning to subside now. I wasn't ready for it. I wasn't prepared.

He spotted me from his side of the crowd. He must have been aware that I was looking right at him; right through him. In the here and now, I could be honest with myself and admit I could not stand the thought of him.

He returned my gaze with a curious expression, like I amused him, like I was an insect, like I was beneath him, or that's how it felt to me. He walked towards me and it was a walk of truth. We knew where each of us stood in relation to the other. Or at least we should have done.

Before he finally caught up with me, I counted another half-dozen handshakes. Exchanges interchanging between 'hello' and 'you're welcome.' With every one, he pushed closer, looming, filling my vision. There was no horizon behind him, only the memory of it. He was Superman having been told that the world had run out of Kryptonite.

He stood in front of me. We did not shake hands. It wasn't as if I'd normally choose to do such a thing—or not do such a thing—but I made it my choice anyway.

'DS Spencer,' he said.

'DI,' I said. 'No stick?'

'Good days, bad days.' He looked back over his shoulder. A hearse was on the approach, winding its way to the burial lot. 'Look, I was talking to the Chief Superintendent. He wants results. We're all under pressure, I know. He needs this whole affair put away before the Climate Change Conference. He's preparing to unleash the dogs of war and he wants me at the head of things. And I want you, DS, on the team.'

'Aye...' I said, and I pinched my nose. What I really wanted to say was *Why*.

Before I had the chance to correct myself, he had already moved off, hand outstretched, in readiness of weaving through the crowd again. As way of assuming his rightful position, appointed by God, closer to the coffin.

And far from me.

***

Pallbearers dressed in uniform and white gloves walked in unison. They held aloft the coffin at shoulder height, the weight of the world on them, the privilege of the living to honour the dead.

Watching on, I was aware of moisture forming on my left nostril. I wiped it away with the dorsal of my hand, then lowered it, then looked down. There was a red smear which wasn't there before. I kept my head down. To the casual onlooker it seemed like I was lost in prayer. Perhaps I was participating in a type of prayer, a conversation, addressing something that wasn't there. But I wasn't conversing with God or some deity. For the answer, you had to start digging and go much lower than that.

'Did you KNOW her?' he said.

'One of our own,' I said.

'YEAH, "*one of our own*", I hear that time and time again. If I was to refer to the HANDS that steal for me, or peddle shit for me, or get fucked for me, as "*one of our own*", I could do it, my conscience as clear as spring water. Yeah, yeah, but don't ask me to CRY crocodile tears for them. They belonged to me, but I had NOTHING to do with them. I only KNEW them if they'd pissed me off enough and I had their ankles separated from their feet. Or had them THROWN off a tall building.'

'And you'd stare into their eyes as they fell.'

'LIKE I did with you.'

'And what did you see?'

'I SAW the Big Man, and I'm left wondering when you're going to let him out again?'

'That part of me is dead.'

'HMPH,' remarked the disembodied voice of Bryce Coleman. There followed a long pause. At least it was an extended pause for him. 'It's YOUR funeral.'

I was back in the real world, and I looked up and sniffed. I sniffed with meaning. My nose was empty and dry, enough to convince me it had stopped bleeding.

The coffin passed the guard of honour and all were saluting, myself included. I was aware that the Chief Superintendent was at the end of the line.

'About to UNLEASH the dogs of war?'

'What did you expect?' I said, now back in my head. 'We'll hit them hard and keep hitting them until someone talks. There will be armed units. Every available resource.'

'Of course, the MEDIA expects a knee jerk reaction, so let's not disappoint. I can understand the NEED for it all to settle down before the Big Show. I get the fact that this is all a PR EXERCISE.'

'That's not how it works,' I protested.

'THAT'S HOW THE WORLD WORKS!' he countered. His voice was like a crack of thunder bouncing around the inside of my skull.

I didn't see the point in arguing back. I'd already guessed we'd have to agree to disagree on many, many things. 'I've been given license to do my own thing,' I said. 'Follow my own leads. It doesn't have to be concrete, more a case of following my instincts.'

'You NEVER came to my funeral.'

'I had an excuse. Would you have wanted me there anyway?'

The coffin was lowered on wooden struts which covered the open grave. Unsurprisingly, a priest was in attendance, his apparel providing a shock of purple against an achromatic backdrop. Silence passed through every individual in the crowd. You could feel it, like it was a presence, an extension of ourselves. That aspect of all of us lost to thought and consumed by memory. But even in the silence, there are voices trying to break out, manifestations of remorse, remembrance, happiness, distress, anger. These are the ghosts that exist in the real world, but only within ourselves.

I never knew Ruth Cairns. Perhaps at some point we'd happen to be in the same room as each other, disparate parts of the same investigation. Perhaps she followed up on a crime report I was too busy to deal with. I never knew her, but at a time like this the least I could do was remember her all the same.

The priest was talking, reading a passage from the Good Book, emoting the mercy of God Almighty and His everlasting love; the indistinguishable states of life and death. The committing of the soul to Heaven and the body to the ground. Even if you didn't believe in a higher being or in an afterlife, it could still be a shared experience, you could still take comfort from the words. You didn't need to know the intimate workings of the Bible to go with the flow.

I could not move, even if I wanted to. I was trapped among the other mourners, transfixed and immobilised by the stark realisation of the sparsity of existence. One environment changed into another. Where mourners had surrounded me by virtue of their free will, I was now flanked by cages which represented the opposite once more. The priest's words were slowly replaced by the echo of metal. I was back in the Bar-L. Once I took my leave of Michael, the mess I was in, I discovered I was bleeding back there too. Back in the corridor, in the company of the prison guard, I noticed a spot of blood on my shoe. There was no sign of any other kind of emission which, considering the state of my damaged hand, was miracle enough.

Horse Peter was dead. Though it seems that before his demise he had got through to someone else. Someone like-minded. Horse Peter had passed something of himself on, like it was a legacy, or an infection. The links of a chain. A nightmare following you, and it's still there, it's behind you, even past the point you awake.

The timeline fit. Three years ago, Horse Peter was found dead in a Bar-L shower. Two years ago, a prisoner named Peter McGarvey, having completed a sentence for armed robbery, was released under licence. But you could make any timeline fit if you had enough wriggle room. And if you were prepared to wriggle.

I crouched down and with my good hand I wiped my shoe clean. I straightened up and took my leave of the guard (having assured him a second time I'd banged my hand on the table by mistake) and continued on my way to the prison doctor.

Yes, it would only have been three years ago Horse Peter fell and cracked his head wide open, leaving behind a big red mark on a wet, greasy wall for his troubles. It was a genuine accident, apparently. I checked, there was no one with him when he died. At least not physically. You could say, as way of putting it out there, that the mind had done its work. It had secured itself a willing disciple, so what further use a body?

And of WPC Ruth Cairns and PC Ryan Patterson? These were not random killings. There had to be a connection. If not this, then what else? This was the only connection I had. Blood merging with water. A second Peter. He was out there somewhere, continuing Horse Peter's work.

And from Bryce Coleman at this time of all times, as if by way of confirmation, there wasn't a peep.

'Ashes to ashes.'

The wooden struts were removed and the pallbearers lowered the coffin into the ground. Each pallbearer gripped onto their cord, lowering the casket four feet, five feet, until the point to let the straps go. The transference from this life to what lay after was never meant to be difficult. Not physically and not spiritually. Only the addition of human emotions could threaten to make it otherwise.

The funeral of PC Ryan Patterson was to take place tomorrow.

Later today, as he talked to the media, I would be at the Chief Superintendent's side. None of the questions directed at me would mean anything. Each would constitute little more than an afterthought. When replying, I would take the Super's lead. I'd carefully parrot what was said previously. It was the things I wouldn't say that were important.

Fifteen years ago, I walked into a stable in Tannoch and, in the poor light, stumbled upon a broken horse robbed of its face. And now, a third of a life later, the image was foremost in my mind, so strong and so vivid the picture could have been taken yesterday. Everything was connected, but it couldn't stay connected for long.

'Dust to dust.'

13.

Carpobrotus

I dreamed of Peter dreaming of me. It didn't matter what dream was what, which dream was which. In the dream, he had the face of a horse and I had the face of a pig. Everything seemed real, the patterns, the colours, except that in either dream, no matter how much we try to reach out, we cannot touch the other's face.

I opened my eyes, surprised momentarily that they had ever been closed. It was time for me to join the unreal world. I called it this because I didn't recognise it. I didn't recognise any of it. For me, my only reality was my flat, positioned as it was at the top of the city. A feeling reinforced by the hard concrete presence beneath my feet. Decorated by the flimsiest of carpeting, no finesse, but never diminished by it. Around me, I had so many notes. Foolscap, Post-its, newspaper, beer mats, anything I could write on. Sometimes I'd make notes on my arms and legs but forget to look there. If I could have I would write on my shadow.

But the call for me to leave had been festering for days now. It had exploded with a sense of purpose alien to my wellbeing. It tightened the gums around my teeth and gave me cramps. It became unbearable. The reality of my room was no longer enough to give me purpose. I needed to expand my reality. You see, the real becomes the unreal. Looking down from afar, all these stories high, I picked a house from down below at random, although once I'd picked it, it could no longer be random. I would have written it down somewhere.

I needed to become a tunnel rat and escape this place I called home.

My front door was unlocked. There was the strong possibility of other inhabitants in other flats, but I was certain none were this high up. This had proved to be a lifesaver in some ways. I hated the idea of breathing in another person's air. I feared if I spent too long in their company, they would contaminate my lungs. My lungs would break down and refuse to work. And not long after, there'd be the rest of me; I would break down and refuse to work. I was terrified of lying down helpless in a corner, the notion of something invisible to the naked eye squeezing the life out of me.

Sometimes, though, someone would climb all the way up to check on me and they'd say, 'Roy Lichtenstein sent me'. But they wouldn't stay for long.

I put on my balaclava, my second skin. Perhaps it

had now become my first. I put my claw hammer in my Bag for Life, along with my pig mask and some strips of gum. Chewing gum furiously to the point it made my ears pop helped me think. I still had a revolver, fully loaded, and a machete occupying a space at the bottom of the wardrobe. Even so, I'd come to a decision: no weaponry from Army & Navy Surplus to accompany me this time. I'd come down against a repeat of the unwieldly pyrotechnics of last time.

I was on my way but I couldn't trust the lifts, ramshackle and fallen into disrepair like much of the rest of the building. In the corridor, what paint there was—a not reassuring grey—was flaking off the walls. The carpet was threadbare and unforgiving. You could spot the patches from the shafts of light which cut a swathe through the general darkness. Where the light came from, I had no idea. I tiptoed to the middle of the corridor, thinking all the while how deliberately obtuse I was being. I stood in front of a door I had passed through many times. I took the claw of the hammer to the lock. The door splintered, then crunched, as I prised it open. I had forced my way in many times before, but I couldn't resist doing my best to put the lock back together, and in my own way fix it, on my return.

But the lock was now very much a casualty of the law of diminishing returns. This latest time, I couldn't help noticing that the lock, and much of the wood around it, was busted. I knew if I dwelled on this, the thought would follow me around; it would trouble me, but close by there was a handily placed distraction. Inside the flat, there was a hole in the floor.

I stood at the edge of the opening. Such was the size of the hole, it looked like a bathtub had fallen through. But this wasn't the bathroom, and this wasn't a bygone time where you might expect a bath in the main room, so I had to put it down to degradation and decay, the receding of floorboards. All around, there were patches of damp the size of small animals. Black mould streaked up the walls. No one could live here, even if they wanted to. And evidence of life had been expedited many moons ago. If anything was left behind, furniture, fittings, a tattered old sofa, it was because it was unwanted.

And me, I was left behind too.

I was passing through. I dropped my Bag for Life through the hole. Weighed down by the hammer, the bag orchestrated a thud against the carpet below. I lowered onto my haunches and swooped down through the gap. My body was perfectly still, except for the falling, as it landed knees first on a dilapidated but padded couch. I bounced off, expending momentum, and before I knew it, I was rolling on the floor. I came to a stop just before a copse of Carpobrotus; ground creeping plants with sharp purple petals. They had become a familiar sight in an otherwise inhospitable expanse, springing from discarded cracked flowerpots, spewing forth a trail of soil like trails of gunpowder, which allowed them to germinate among the cracks in the floor and tears in the carpet and thus extend their reach. Sometimes I'd give them water.

Carpobrotus does not originate from Scotland, which made me think the flat's last occupant was an amateur botanist. Although I did not know the occupant, I couldn't help but consider them a kindred spirit, being an amateur something myself. Although my passion was taxidermy.

Extracts of Carpobrotus mixed with water could be used to treat diarrhoea and stomach cramps. This would have been a fact that we could have shared, if only we'd known each other.

I retrieved the bag and continued on my way. Directly across from the flat was the fire escape, which allowed unfettered access to fourteen floors down. I descended the steps, the worn heels of my shoes slapping against the stairs, the hard surface. There was no give, I felt every vibration from every point of impact shoot up and coalesce around my calves.

After this, it got more difficult. The encountering of a series of derelict, closed places. Down I'd go through a series of apertures, dragging the bag behind me. Through cladding, beams and piping, turning and spinning like a drill, accumulating dust, my feet hitting solid ground many times over. Slowly navigating past something jutting out, metal snagging the clothes on my back. Dirty water in my hair, trickling around my ears. Sometimes it was hard breathing through the mask, making my breath uncomfortably warm, but I wouldn't have it any other way.

As I descended, I was aware of noise, clanking and scraping. It was the noise of movement. The noise of life. At this point, the probability of people still in the flats below would get real. Congregating on the lower floors, I had no way of knowing if, unlike me, they were original residents. Forcing their way in, despite the (admittedly light) security, to make use of the vacated rooms. We were all rats in a maze and I worried that such activity would bring unwarranted attention, but that was me being paranoid. Which was a good thing. There was virtue to be had in such a state of mind. It kept you alert.

Eventually, I would succumb to the interrupted gravity. I reached the corridor which announced I was on the ground floor. Looking across the hall, I spotted a shoeless boy. He was standing outside the door of one of the flats to my right. The boy was not confused as such, but still, he seemed uncertain what to do. One of his hands was clenched; perhaps trying to decide if he should knock on the door. Or not, I don't know. His clothes were dirty. He turned his head as he saw me too. I put a vertical finger to my mouth and he followed suit. I turned the handle of the door to the left of me, which acquiesced easily in my grip. With that, I took my leave of the shoeless boy.

The flat—the latest flat upon flat upon flat—was empty inside. There was something that looked a lot like excrement smeared on the walls. Strewn on the floor were sheets of newspaper and empty glass bottles. None of the bottles were intact, an opportune reminder to stay nimble on one's feet. At the far wall was an outside window, closed and with the latch attached.

The window was large enough to accommodate my not considerable bulk. The glass was cracked, and inundated with cobweb, but it held firm. Having lifted the latch, having opened it carefully, I used my arms to bear my weight and lever me up and out. On the other side, my body spooled outwards, forming a makeshift belly flop. I threw out my arms and extended my body, piecing together an inelegant handstand. My hands made contact with a thatch of weeds and grass. I used uninterrupted gravity to uncoil and restore equilibrium, returning to a standing position. I took a moment to normalise. I could feel in my bones that the temperature was dipping, which made for a harsh evening. There I was, exposed to the elements, taking several breaths, waiting for my body to cool, and my insides to settle.

I knew where I was going. When I saw the house from up on high, it had set off a burning feeling in my chest and stomach, a reflux reaction which would not subside until I had formed the conviction to do what was needed to be done. It was the only part of the outside world which now interested me. I had been on recon previously. I knew what to expect when I got there.

Out here, the wearing of the balaclava was too conspicuous. There had been several police statements already, appealing for information from the public, releasing my description, referring to me as the Balaclava Man, or The Man in the Ski Mask, or simply as The Man. No choice but to take it off or all of this would be in vain, even though, without fail, this would mean the worst feeling in my life. It hardly seemed worth it. I laid a hand on the wall behind me and waited for the flats to lean forward and slide off its foundations. For the building to collapse and reduce my body to a smear. But this did not happen, even though part of me wanted it to.

I let go. I peeled it like the skin of a grape, conscious I was the grape. Bypassing the Bag of Life, I slid the balaclava inside my jacket and I held my hand in close to keep it in place.

I started walking. When people passed, or before it came to that, having already registered them on my people radar, it came down to playing it by instinct. I stepped to the side and turned my head and lifted my hand and obscured my face, and that would have to do. I reminded myself that the world at ground level was no different to the one seen from the air. It was all a matter of perspective. And then it was gone, taking the shape of an elongated blur, my awareness of time.

***

I lifted the baby monitor in front of me. It was shaped like a toy walkie talkie. My intention was to whisper into it, but out of nowhere a hacking cough leapt from my mouth. The child in its cot beside me slept like a lamb, as it had done when I crawled in from the cold through the bedroom window minutes before. From one window back in the Flats to another here in Cathcart Road.

I could hear movement from the bottom of the stairs, then the shuffle of footsteps, a compromise of speed and sound, culminating in movement up the stairs. I was back in my balaclava.

The bedroom door swung slowly open. The fact that such an undertaking was so drawn out was surprising, amounting to an eerily quiet transaction. It was almost a blessing when in stepped the mother. Her hand still on the door handle, she stood as motionless as the child in its bed. The side of my face twitched, although she wasn't to know that, obscured as it was by the mask. Her eyes darted around the room, moving fitfully from my mask to the baby to the Bag for Life resting on the carpet. And finally, to the open window where the net curtains swayed in the wind in an understated way. For a second, going on two, neither of us were breathing.

The father appeared moments later, rushing past his partner; his spouse, I could see, by placement of the rings. He headed straight towards me. I raised the palm of one hand. With my second hand I clutched the top of the cot. My grip on the guard was tight, my knuckles whitening.

The father stopped in his tracks, the air leaving his lungs, which left him breathless as well.

I was the only one moving. I took my claw hammer and pig mask out of the bag. My movements were slow, almost slow motion. A mercy of sorts as it allowed the parents to adjust to the situation they now found themselves in. I draped the pig mask over the side of the cot.

I made a twirling motion with my finger, instructing them to turn towards the wall. The father, understanding immediately, grabbed the mother's arm a little roughly, ensuring their joint cooperation. And about they turned. The mother was weeping softly now. 'Please, please, please,' she uttered under her breath.

'No,' I said, 'You don't have a voice. Ah've taken that from you.'

I was in another place. Taken on another journey. Another adventure. I swear when I turned my head, I could hear him whisper in my ear.

I took a breath. 'Ah love our little family,' I said, this time in a squeaky tinny voice.

'Ah love our little family,' I repeated, but this time in a deep, boomy voice. 'I am so fankful for it.'

'But fings change,' I said, in what I recognised to be my true voice. 'People change. They have to.'

I walked forward and swung the hammer, which connected, jarring with the mother's neck and shoulder. She crumpled, but not before slamming her forehead against the wall. Despite this, she was still moving on the ground, disorientated, attempting to crawl out of the bedroom.

My arm was tight from the elbow down. I couldn't stop my head from shaking. I was deliberating on whether I should hit her again when she stopped moving.

The father lunged into me and I came perilously close to being knocked off my feet. I hit out with the hammer, this time using the claw side, which made impact with his Adam's apple. The momentum of it tore up his throat. It lodged in his jaw.

He fell to his knees, blood bubbling out his nose. I pulled the hammer from him, spattering blood and skin and scattering fragments of bone on the carpet.

The situation had escalated quickly. Too quickly, spoiling my plans. Horse Peter couldn't join me, at least not in any tangible way, so maybe someone else could? I wanted the father to wear the pig mask at the start. I wanted to see if it was up to the task, if it was a good fit. If it changed him before I changed him, like it had changed me. Like I *hoped* it had changed me.

And now his head was slick with a red ooze. His body trembled without purpose as I bore down on his shoulders and I pulled the pig mask down and covered his face. Despite the stickiness, despite the resistance, I tried to do so as uniformly as possible.

And now all of that was gone. There was no power to imbue, there was nothing to see, his strength had already waned.

There was no Horse Peter.

He was trying to say something, a pointless exercise considering the state of his throat and the thickness of the mask wrapped around him. Still, what harm would there be to respond? I could think of only one thing.

'Don't wake the baby,' I said.

I brought the hammer down on the back of his head. Emphatically so. And he lay there next to his wife, two bloody entangled masses. There was nothing revelatory to come from this; nothing of note. I contemplated the husband. I tried to remember why this family had appealed to me so.

He'd changed, that was undeniable, but still, the mask was anything but a good fit.

14.

Halfway Down the Stairs

We approached the crime scene, slowly. Slowly because the DI required his walking stick again. He could not walk, virtually bent over, hobbling, batting away my repeated offers to help.

You could see the high-rise flats, the same flats as before if my bearings weren't off. In the not-too-distant distance, towering over us, and this caused my mind to panic slightly. I was adding two plus two to make, I don't know, eight. I was coming to all kinds of conclusions, a pinball machine set off in my brain. If I couldn't provide physical support, maybe I could offer some kind of reassurance instead.

'Victoria Flats aren't going to be standing for long. I checked. Up for demolition. All part of the plan to regenerate the area. Residents have been rehoused already.' I wasn't sure if the DI was even listening. And I was wondering why I was giving a damn anyway when twenty-four hours ago I couldn't even look him in the eye. Still, I continued, 'The last resident to be cleared out was old Hughie, remember him? He held up a chip shop in the Gorbals for a bag of fish and chips. He claimed a banana in his pocket was a gun.'

The DI straightened up some, a little hunched still but, as stances go, nothing as dramatic as before. The main reason for this seemed less to do with me and more to do with the officer standing outside the crime scene, a residential property in Cathcart Road. The officer noticeably straightened up as well, prelude to giving a salute. It wasn't subtle, the salute was exclusively for the DI. I was just along for the ride.

'At ease, PC Garland,' the DI said. 'Your Uncle Rufus feeling better? Pneumonia, was it?'

'Thanks, Sir,' PC Garland said. 'Turned out it was blood clot on the lung. Could have gone one way or the other. Thanks for asking, Sir.'

'Oh,' DI said, 'ah.'

'In recovery though. Over the worst of it.'

'I'm glad to hear it.'

'It's okay to enter, Sir. Forensics are about to wrap things up.'

'Cheers.'

***

The incident had occurred in the child's bedroom, so that's where I was headed. There followed the soft, uncertain tread of two feet on each stair, followed by the periodic thump of wood. The odd grunt thrown in for free. I was disappointed to the point of dismay at the amount of effort even a simple task like climbing a flight of stairs was turning out to be, but still I ploughed on. What was the alternative? To stop? To wither away? To get myself to the glue factory?

And then I remembered my manners. 'Sorry, I wasn't ignoring you there,' I said. 'Just a bit preoccupied. Not feeling quite 100%. I'm fine, just more war wounds than I can count. Just don't be expecting push ups. Your views, your opinions, they are very important to me. If anything, I've to come to depend...'

My neck was creaking, testament to looking back over my shoulder, only to find DS Spencer wasn't there. She hadn't followed me in. And there I was alone, talking to myself as it turned out. What was the alternative? You had to have at least one course of action in the bank before examining the possibility of another.

I looked around. I was halfway up the stairs, which could also mean I was halfway down.

***

My mind, my whole thought process, was sluggish. On the approach, I had to shorten my stride to keep in line with the DI to the point it didn't feel comfortable, it didn't feel right, and that's all it took apparently to turn my brain to mush. Then at the door he had a quick conversation with the PC and I was reminded just how accomplished a people person he was. He was an oddball, but a good conversationalist. He entered the house in that discombobulated style of his, leaving me too slow to react, almost rooted to the spot.

'PC Garland,' I said.

'Ma'am,' he said.

'Sorry to hear about your uncle,' I said, and he gave me a look. It was a number of looks actually, his eyes flitting all over the place, but every one of them said, *please not this conversation again.*

There was a sound, which came from behind me. I turned to survey the front garden, a perfectly functional front garden. At first sight nothing out of the ordinary. A large privet hedge squared off the garden. The hedge was overgrown, a mass of meshed green leaves. I stood perfectly still, my ears straining, picking up only empty space.

'You hear that?'

'Hear what?'

There it was again. Definitely a sound.

A tiny sound, high-pitched, intense, ephemeral, carried half-heartedly by the breeze.

'That, you hear that?'

'Hear what?' PC Garland said again. The difference here was his voice, conveying exasperation levels on the rise.

I was none the wiser, but my brain was waking up. What to do? What to do?

There was little point asking PC Garland.

Time to investigate.

***

The uneven traction I was having difficulty mastering receded at incline's end. At the top of the landing, I was met by a man in a hairnet and white jumpsuit. Everything about him screamed scrubbed, sterile, incredibly clean. It hollered forensics. The type who went about his work while bringing absolutely nothing of the outside world with him.

'Hammond,' he said.

'Fisher,' I said.

The bedroom door was ajar. Among the patches of blood was a single body.

'Assailant came at two adults with a hammer, I'd say. One female, a Susan Cowan, one male, a Samuel Cowan,' Hammond said. 'On discovery of the bodies—a grandparent I believe, helping with childcare—the woman was found breathing. She was rushed to ICU. Male wasn't so lucky.'

'I can see that,' I said. My gaze fell on the corpse. It always felt strange to discuss a person's demise when their body was still in the room. Not that this was something you were ever supposed to get used to. From my vantage point, there was a red raw hole occupying the back of his head.

'The first blow was around the neck area,' Hammond continued. 'A second, probably fatal blow then applied to the back of the head. I found latex fragments embedded in the back of the skull. A party mask I'd say. An adult one. The type they might have a use for at a Halloween party, covers the head and neck. Pretty pliable to withstand a blow of that force. No sign of the mask at the crime scene. Killer either put the mask on the victim, or took it off, or both probably. Again, with force. There's light bruising around the neck. The least of the victim's problems.'

Connections connected connecting...

'You think there's a connection with the incident at Shawlands Drive?' I asked, quickly, too quickly. 'Except the mask was on the perpetrator and now a mask on the victim?'

'You're the detective,' he said.

I stepped into the bedroom and was greeted with a chill which made me think of Hell frozen over, and then of East Kilbride in January. 'Window is open,' I said.

'You ask me, assailant came in through the window, then left through the front door. Neighbours heard nothing, so the attacker knew what they were doing. The door was unlocked, confirmed by the grandparent. She doesn't live far from here apparently.'

'Another detective is interviewing the grandmother,' I said. 'Probably over a cup of tea and a custard cream,' I added perhaps a little too wistfully. I liked this Hammond. I appreciated his straight talking. I wasn't aware if I'd encountered him before. 'Anything unusual?'

'You mean besides one dead, one fighting for her

life?' he said, with no hint of irony in his voice. 'There was a Post-it note seemingly discarded on the floor near the husband. Unusual, a combination of lines and random letters, but we'll take a look at it.'

'Oh, and last of all, there was this.' He held up a small clear sealed bag. Inside, slightly crushed around the edges, was a purple flower. 'There's no evidence of this or any other kind of flower anywhere else around the house.'

Not that I'm any expert, but it wasn't a tulip or a sunflower, wasn't one I readily recognised. 'Where was it?'

'On the cot. Killer might have inadvertently brought it in with him on his clothes. Although it's a big flower, hardly not noticeable. He might have left it there on purpose. Might very well have nothing to do with the case. Not much to go on, but we'll check it out back in the lab.'

I said, 'Can I give you my number? Keep me updated?'

He nodded and I slowly enunciated my private mobile number, and he studiously added each digit to his contacts.

'Good,' he said. 'Sorted. Not a problem. Do you want mine?'

'If it's okay, I'd rather not, thanks.'

I approached the cot, which was empty except for a shawl carefully folded and laid out on the mattress.

'Where's the baby?' I asked.

He didn't answer straight away.

'No baby at the crime scene,' he said at last. 'I thought you guys were dealing with that.'

I pointed meekly at the baby monitor. 'Baby monitor?' I said, rather redundantly.

'Purely audio feed. Dusted for prints, but assuming the perpetrator wore gloves, it won't tell us anything.' At this point, Hammond was already trotting down the stairs. 'I'll give you a minute,' he called back. 'Don't step on anything!'

I was alone, a body without a pulse not-withstanding. I stood for a second in a room once brimming with life and hope and bright colours now cut down by brutality, the violence of murder.

'You still have YOUR hammer?' And there it was, the voice of Bryce Coleman.

'How do you know about that?'

'Oh, fuck I know EVERYTHING. Detective Inspector FISHER is quite the legend in my kind of circles. Quite the BOGEYMAN. Word GETS around. You, with your hammer safely TUCKED away underneath your pillow.'

'Not anymore. It was spirited away in an evidence bag a year ago, just before the fall. I used it to protect myself against a dog.'

'BIG dog?'

'I thought you knew everything.'

'BIG DOG?'

'The biggest. Now I think about it, they took away my diary as well; still waiting on them to replace it. And my flask too.'

'Is THIS your man?' he said. We had moved away from the topic of man's best friend (there were notable exceptions) back to the matter at hand. The nature of the killer. The nature of the killing.

'I don't know. Forensics should confirm one way or the other.'

'But what does your GUT say?'

I had long since come to terms with the necessity of listening to my gut. It had a lot to say for itself. I was looking for patterns, not forgetting that the mother was still breathing in a hospital ward somewhere, but pushing this to one side. Staring at an empty skull. Staring at the congealed blood on the carpet, adjusting to the fact that this was no longer a nursery, but a crime scene. To divine some meaning, and in so doing, come to some sort of conclusion. It didn't matter how removed the thought processes I applied were from the logical or sane.

'Incident at Shawlands Drive. Immobilises the female first, skins the male. Leaves a note definitely. Here, immobilises the female first, covers the male's face with a mask, bludgeons him to death. Leaves a note maybe. Sex of the victims is irrelevant. The act of killing incidental. The method of attack premeditated, even if the consequences were not.'

'All fucking GREEK to me.'

'Amount of force used suggests the perpetrator is male. Can he express himself in any other way? Product of a predominantly male environment.'

'Like a BOARDING school?'

'Like a prison.'

I had dreamed of him. Not of him, but of the one who came before him. I could have said that, articulated this, but I didn't want to muddy the waters. I didn't want to make this all about lineage. About succession. He did not want to be him, but even so, on the way to changing into something else, he could do nothing to prevent him from becoming him.

'He making a STATEMENT, then? Caught up in some TRANSFORMATION bollocks. You'd KNOW all about that. Serial KILLERS are not my forte. There's no PROFIT margin in them. Not enough RETURN on your investment. The type of BAMPOT even I can't use. NOT really.'

'He has a code. A simple one. One that is easy to remember. He writes things down. Let's give him the benefit of the doubt. It keeps him right. It keeps him from not becoming too muddled.'

'No, not a statement,' I continued, 'not a transformation. Projecting himself as someone else, or on someone else, so he can ask the question and be in a position where he can understand the answer. The question I think we all ask at some point in our life, while not going anywhere near the extremes of our perpetrator, while not resulting in such problematic and tragic consequences. He's asking—'

'Who am I?'

I was surrounded by chaos, but there was one oasis in among the turmoil. The baby's cot. I felt drawn to it. The shawl on the mattress was symmetrical and perfectly central. It no longer belonged here in this room. Too pure. Too fragile. I reached down and laid a hand flat on the mattress and, put this down to a vivid imagination, could feel the warmth from it.

***

I crept up to the hedge, almost on my tiptoes. To any unfortunate onlooker (prominently PC Garland) I must have looked like I'd lost all my marbles. I'd lost some other people's marbles as well. There was no cry, but there was some definite rustling coming from inside the hedge. The image of a bird building a nest popped into my head. Undeterred, I plunged my arms into the shrub, using the back of my hands to push apart the branches. Scrambling beyond the daunting, twisted undergrowth, there was more empty space.

I came into contact with something soft and diminutive and did my best to lift it out without snagging, without the hedge reclaiming it as its own. I kept at it, lifting, adjusting, checking, until the object was free of the hedge, mustering my remaining strength, drawing on everything in my power not to drop it.

Drop *him*. A young boy. Not quite a baby, not quite a toddler. His face was filthy, there was dirt along the cuffs of his baby grow. Carefully I lifted the boy to my ear. My ears, already at straining point, asked to push on some more.

There was a faint wheeze, a mixture of breathing and snoring, the product of an infant's lungs, the nasal passage. He was sleeping like babies do. He was dreaming. He was alive.

'The baby. Good work, Detective.' A voice came from the front gate. The gate, not wishing to be left out, squeaked as it swung on metal hinges.

Standing there, having walked along the garden path, was a man in a hairnet and white jumpsuit.

'The best,' I said, allowing myself a smile. I was up on my tiptoes. It was a time of other emotions. Of hope, and of a little joy. Ones I hadn't felt in a very long time.

15.

Magical Mystery Tour

The funerals were over and war was declared against the criminal fraternity. How is war declared in such circumstances? We hit the most visible targets hard. We hit everyone we know who has dirty fingers. We put on a show of maximum effect in the sure knowledge we inflict only flesh wounds. It only takes scratching under the surface for us to realise that scratching is all we are capable of. And with such a rousing endorsement still ringing in our ears, it was off to war we go.

Overtime flowed like water. Dawn raids; raids at dusk. There was no official confirmation, we'd keep the media silent on that one, but we couldn't stop the rumours surrounding the mutilation of Cairns and Patterson spreading like wildfire. It was a cloudy day when we descended on a residential estate which consisted of ex-council houses, semi-detached, now privately owned. A door, recently given a fresh lick of paint, crumbled under a police-wielded battering ram. The battleship grey of the exterior now given way to bright, dazzling light, creating a neon yellow shimmer that enveloped a green, green sea.

A half dozen police officers held their hands up to their foreheads in unison, and kept them there until their pierced eyes grew accustomed to the vicious glare. Once they did so, they realised they'd stepped into two houses, the wall which once separated them knocked down.

They'd walked into a jungle. A forest of triangular shaped trees. A cannabis farm. There was a door at the far wall, the unmistakable smell informing us that it led to a makeshift toilet. One of the officers was leading out a guy in overalls, hands cuffed behind him. The guy in overalls seemed disinterested, the reality of being taken into custody one of the hazards of the job. Then his face lit up as he thought of something to say.

'Officer, a word,' he said. 'I counted you in. You're missing two.'

The officer hardly broke stride as he pushed Overalls with force into the wall.

'Shut it,' the officer instructed the crumpled mess in front of him.

It was all terribly perfunctory. It was all part of the dance. The officer resumed escorting Overalls out. The officer gave me a thumbs up as he passed.

'Good tip off, Sir,' he said.

The Super had promised we'd come down on them like a ton of bricks, and I had my inside man. A voice whispered in my ear—from inside my ear.

'NEXT stop *Buff Tub*,' the voice said.

I said, 'The *what what?*'

Fortunately, the voice was prepared to divulge an address.

The Buff Tub was just off St Vincent Street, Glasgow city centre. It was a basement location, you had to go down stone steps to access it. It was literally a *popup* establishment. A shelf life of days. Years in the planning, months in the preparation, less than a week in the execution, before everything—the whole kit and kaboodle—was moved on. It was a massage parlour where anything—absolutely anything—goes. Escape rooms with no chance of escape, not for the victims, where sex trafficking was one example of many crimes perpetrated upon them.

A horrifying smorgasbord of all ages, all ethnicities, all sexes. Used and abused as a matter of course and taken in and out again in bags. An unholy mixture of blood and semen washed at regular intervals off soundproofed walls.

Everything was planned far in advance, the various locations vetted and approved at the highest level, and '*guests*' of such establishments were willing to pay a king's ransom for the privilege. It was capitalism, raw, unadulterated and unfiltered. It was at its greatest which meant it was at its worst. It was the prosecution case for the destruction of humanity all gathered helpfully under one roof.

Hidden in plain sight, because frankly this type of thing did not happen. It might have happened somewhere else maybe, some faraway foreign land, but not here. Never here. The length and breadth of it too awful to ever try to contemplate. Which begged the question, how did I know so much about it? Its present location, the activities inside? It felt like I was drawing on more than intuition. Were there latent memories shifting inside my mind? My mind with so many layers, many of which I had since disowned. Many I had purged, subjected to my own personal scorched earth policy. I didn't want to think about that. Didn't want to go back there. But to be surrounded by so much sickness and contamination, to breathe it in and then hold my breath, how long before I then get sick again?

'Is this your doing? You approved this?'

'Nothing so CRASS, but it was my business to be aware of it.'

I watched (we watched) as the firearms unit descended.

Me and the walking stick, we'd follow them in, but only when safe to do so, once given the all-clear. The officers using what feet were meant for—to kick down doors. Their various shouts giving way to various screams from the various occupants. A single shot was fired, splitting the evening air in two.

'How can you stand it?'

'When all you've known as a child is how to eat SHIT, you learn to stomach anything.'

'And now?'

'And now I want you to TORCH it. RAZE it to the fucking ground. Lead all those motherfuckers out and have THEM assassinated. FUCK them.' I could see him turn and grin at me inside my head. His features were chalk white. There was no warmth around his face, no life behind his eyes. Just a forsaken steeliness. A declaration of damnation. 'The WAR, my friend, has just got real.'

Except he was no friend of mine. He was a voice, a manifestation, from inside me. And nothing good tended to come from inside me.

The raid of the Buff Tub would keep the authorities and TARA busy for a long time. And it didn't end there. There followed long nights, as many night raids as we could fit into the designated time period. Drug factories, slum landlords, as many last known addresses of the usual suspects as could be mustered. All courtesy of Strathclyde's finest, on a magical mystery tour. None of the subsequent targets proving as big a prize as the Buff Tub though, but Bryce Coleman had already made his mark. If he had any more irons in the fire, which he surely did, he now chose to keep his own counsel.

And it was over. If not a ceasefire, then a temporary reprieve. I felt sunlight on my skin for the first time in ages.

I returned to my apartment. It was mid-afternoon

and I had been awake for over twenty-four hours, but sleep was the last thing on my mind.

My mind had blown a circuit somewhere. The transmission of pain, the signal crossing the spinal cord, was no longer getting through to my brain. From the previous confines of my body, there was no debilitating discomfort. There was nothing of the sort. Where before there were good days and bad days, I was sure for the most part that this was all over. Only the former lay ahead. I was feeling like I was a new man. And this worried me greatly.

Right there and then, I could have done fifty push-ups. I could have blown up a hundred balloons then, biting each and every one of them, made them go pop. But that would cross the line. Every neuron I called my own would be setting off an alarm. It was too close. Too close for comfort. Too close to aping my former *self*, which was the last thing I wanted. In terms of need, this bumped sleep into second place. Even the prospect of good days could have negative connotations.

Was this to be my life now, to live in fear of anything that would smack of the unexpected, the extroverted? To live in fear of *him* still, even now? I thought I had won, and I needed to keep thinking this, reminding myself of this, because it had to mean something. It had to be true.

Physically at this point I was in fine fettle. In as good a shape as I could ever realistically hope for. My head, though, was still playing catch-up. So, it wouldn't be wide of the mark to suggest the last thing I wanted was a chat. It was another thing to add to the list. That said, as sleep was the only other option currently, and realistically, open to me, I decided I couldn't keep putting off asking the question I knew I'd have to ask eventually. And so, reluctantly, I acquiesced.

I said, 'Why are you helping with all this?'

He said, 'Your monkey balls, I've TOLD you why.'

'You've told me what you want, I've had plenty of that, but you haven't told me why.'

'WHY "WHY?" Always the fucking questions, always the fucking DETECTIVE, what does it matter why? I'm giving you a free HAND here. No strings ATTACHED. It just IS, that's all.'

He grew quiet after this, as did I. We had reached an impasse, me and the voice inside my head. I had no control over this, and in truth I probably never had. It was the illusion of control that risked being shattered. I closed my eyes and when I opened them again a full minute had passed.

'OK,' he said eventually. 'Let's TALK. Come INTO my office.'

I accepted his invitation. It called for a mental shift, the entering of a familiar room. There were no windows, the room felt stuffy. Smells, welcome or not, familiar or not, lingered here. Bryce Coleman stood behind his table, arms folded, like he owned the place. I couldn't protest too much. This was a part of my mind I certainly had no claim to.

Coleman unentangled himself from the picture, in

order to first pour and then hand me a glass of whisky. 'To my FAVOURITE missile,' he said. 'A TOAST.'

I looked at the glass, which I circled in my hand. I marvelled at its ridges which were perfectly symmetrical. The only perfectly symmetrical thing about me, maybe. I wondered how many of these I could drink before this part of my mind persuaded the other parts that I was drunk.

He clinked his glass against mine. The sound was as sharp as it was deafening, it brought tears to the eyes. Or maybe that was the whisky.

'To my rise and FALL.' He winked, while still retaining a deadpan expression. 'We all KNOW about my fall.'

'If you're QUESTIONING my motives, nothing I'm going to say will make a difference, but we're here now, so why don't I give you a flavour. Some BRUSHSTROKES.'

'I didn't know my MOTHER and I only met my father many years later when I was a man myself. He was a fucking drunk, near PASSED out in a gutter. I ordered one of my men to HOLD him down and another to prise open his mouth, and I pissed in it. It was a POINTLESS thing to do. IT meant nothing to me, but I did it anyway.'

'Maybe OTHERS have a better relationship with their Daddy. My only REGRET was that I didn't have a bigger bladder.'

'As a YOUTH, I was a spiteful little bastard, institutionalised for most of my childhood. I was the

LUCKY one. I had two SIBLINGS, a brother and sister. The BROTHER was farmed out to a succession of foster homes. The last one was a really austere one, where the PUNISHMENT for his many mis-demeanours was to be made to sleep in a garage on a trampoline. A TRAMPOLINE for Christ sakes. One night when in a DEEP sleep, he fell off and smashed his head off the concrete floor. It was instant, as soon as he hit the concrete, DEAD as a doornail. The family escaped prosecution, but I caught UP with them eventually. One unsolved CASE of arson later...'

'The family that adopted my SISTER emigrated to Australia when she was twelve. Effectively taking her outside my sphere of influence, lucky for them, GOOD for her.'

'I didn't stop my SEARCH there. I found my extended family, made myself KNOWN to them to various degrees. They all KNEW who I was. FAMILY is important. As I went up the ranks, or maybe down the ranks if you prefer, moving from money launderer to trusted enforcer to even more trusted lieutenant, all the way up to boss man—but you know all this, or you'll have a pretty good idea—I needed my family around me to PROVE that, if it came to it, I was prepared to put them in second place. My CRIME family, my real family if you like, came first. If it came to push and shove—If my loyalty was questioned—I'd book them a place on the SACRIFICIAL altar.'

'My GODSON committed suicide. JUMPED off a tall building. Did so to COINCIDE with two genuine executions also scheduled for that day. He was always a SMART cookie that one. His idea of a FUCK YOU, I suppose, because that's what the legend says, I have a liking for that sort of thing. Throwing a fucker from a GREAT height. My FAVOURITE type of execution.'

'More than an urban legend, surely?' Maybe the effects of the whisky had loosened my tongue, but I couldn't help but interject.

'YOU tell me. YOU'RE the expert.' He was frowning now. 'And DON'T call me fucking Shirley.'

'Didn't you HEAR? My GODSON.'

'I'm sorry, my condolences.'

I seemed to have lost focus. I wasn't aware of there being any walls or any floor. We were both standing in an empty blackness. A darkness whichever way you looked at it that was without end. It was just him, me, and a desk. A big wooden desk. If anything, it seemed to have grown in size.

'He was MY godson. He was a nephew TWICE removed. A double WHAMMY.'

'The story put out there was that I ORDERED his killing. Down to PISH-POOR exam results, a drug deal gone wrong, and so on and so on. As IF it didn't matter which one you believed. All that mattered was that it was OUT there. My bloodline couldn't be SEEN to be weak. It was something I could SACRIFICE right enough, but any such perceived failings, any flaws in their nature, this was equally SOMETHING I could not allow to reflect back on me. LIFE in the fast lane. A two-way MIRROR. The LAW of the jungle. My balls ON the line. *Non DUCOR, duco.*'

'A nephew PERMANENTLY removed.'

'When I sent out MY most trusted lieutenants to do my bidding, to be my heralds, I was standing behind a desk not too unlike this one. On the desk was a DECANTER not too unlike the one I have here. And I SIPPED from an identical whisky glass. And I was alone, and there came running down my face, two long streaky TEARS. Two tears only, I would not ALLOW myself the luxury of more. I dug my nails into my palms, drawing blood, and ground my teeth to sawdust and willed myself to STOP fucking crying. *I can cry all I like when I'm dead*, I told myself, repeatedly, until this was all THAT I could think about; *I can cry all I like when I'm dead.*'

'And NOW...'

'And now...'

Was it so different in death as it was in life? I looked upon this bald, hairless creature, his eyebrows so blonde they'd reached the point of translucent. As is customary for a man of granite, his features were carved out of stone. I could not read his face, an empty canvas. Even a smile or a wink were the actions of someone who had unlearned the basic emotions so he could relearn them and so better control them. To never let them betray you, that was the mantra. To become the master inside and out. And now he had shuffled off this mortal coil, there was nothing, there were no tears. Nary a shred of evidence of humanity on display to call his own. An ashen-faced man dressed in a dark suit in a dark room. A ferocious spirit. Dead before his time. He was beyond me.

'Then you KILLED me; you survived, but not before you revealed your—what do you call it—*other self*. And that's just COBBLERS. What would it take to GET the big man back? How many POKES will it take with a shitty stick? Squeeze that stump of yours, drown yourself in an ocean of pus, until HE comes crawling out of the fucking water. Like a FISH becomes a reptile. He's the *real* you, believe me I have an EYE for these things.'

'No, I...'

'And there you go AGAIN with that golem, whiney voice of yours. Honestly, just CAN it. You're a fucking broken RECORD, mate. Everything I built up, all the shit I had to take, what I had to do to fucking get there, to STAY there, you took all this away from me. You OWE me. I never INTENDED this to be a criminal empire to be handed down or fought over. I want it all torn down, and you're the ONE who is going to help me do it.'

Bryce Coleman was animated now. Spittle emanated from his mouth. Maybe I would help him, maybe I wouldn't. It wasn't necessarily my gift to give, but if it came to it, I had my price.

Everyone does, and it would be hopelessly naive to argue otherwise. I was biding my time, at least until the steam went elsewhere other than coming out of his ears. But it occurred to me, I couldn't let him and his mood swings, the extremes, come between me and my own set of priorities.

Didn't I get to decide? Couldn't I be the person I wanted to be? I needed to break away from being cowed by it. I needed to make my voice heard. 'I need help finding the killer,' I said. 'The man in the mask. The Balaclava Man.'

He grew quieter at this, more reflective. The realisation sinking in, as much as he may have wanted it otherwise, that it wasn't all about him.

'We all wear MASKS one way or the other,' he said. 'You ask me, a BALACLAVA is just showing off.'

'They say NATURE abhors a vacuum. *Vacuum sacuum.* Since my unfortunate passing, things have most definitely not gone to SHIT. My fiefdom CONTINUES virtually intact. No infighting, everyone sticking to their assigned roles, no chicanery, no kind of BATSHIT crazy. Which can only mean one thing, BIG ROY has shown an interest.'

'A phrase so seemingly innocuous as *Big Roy*, mention it to HALF the criminals in this city and they'll instantly shit their pants. The other half will BOTH piss and shit themselves. Hell, he was the ONLY one I answered to. The only one any FUCKER answers to.'

'YOU need help on finding the killer.' He pointed a finger at me. 'Of your TWO little boys in blue?'

The finger was perfectly straight. I couldn't think of anything straighter. It took on an even greater prominence when he started twirling it. It was mesmerising, forming circles out of the air. Or its equivalent in this office of his, which would have to be dead air.

'If THAT'S your price, then that's fine by me. We're two HAPPY bunnies bouncing in the ash and muck. All roads LEAD to Roy Lichtenstein, and I will show you the way.'

Bryce Coleman opened his arms as wide as he feasibly could. For a second, I thought he was going to try to sell me a used car or a small nuclear weapon.

'All that is required is that YOU follow.'

16.

Date No. 3

I plonked myself down at the bar. It wasn't the most ladylike of ways to engage with a barstool, I'd be the first to put up my hands and admit. *Plonked, honked, bonked.* I guess I was feeling frisky, uncharacteristically so, but there's a first time for everything I suppose.

'What's your poison?' the barman said.

'My what?'

'Drink?'

'Oh, bottle of Peroni,' I said. 'Please.' I so wanted to call the barman *barkeep* because it reminded me of a comedy sketch that I found hysterical when I was six or seven. What was it from again? One of Dad's old videos. *Russ Abbot's Bad house? Mad spouse? Madhouse?*

It wasn't often that I thought of Dad. He died so young. I couldn't understand my feelings at the time, but I could learn to block them out, and did so in a way that I couldn't do with Mum. And Mum was so many years later. I'm no psychiatrist, but I had developed a block on having a block. With Mum it was the peeling of one layer of grief to reveal the next, and then the next. (Maybe I should talk to someone about this.)

I think I was finally coming down from the euphoria. It was over twenty-four hours ago, the elation of finding a young child alive in a garden hedge. It was an extraordinary moment. It was an affirmation of sorts; that what I was doing wasn't completely pointless. That I wasn't just rearranging furniture. And now I was waiting at a bar for Date No. 3. I had to remind myself of yesterday because today had been a stressful, fractious, cul-de-sac type of day already.

***

While the others were out playing cops and robbers, the DI had entrusted me with the balaclava case. Forensics hadn't yet confirmed a link between the events of Shawlands Drive and Cathcart Road, but this was the DI's main line of enquiry, and it was mine too. The mother from Cathcart Road was in a stable but critical condition, but I still had to sit down with Fiona Murray, primary witness of the incident from Shawlands Drive. Due to the damage to her flat caused by the blast, Murray had been temporarily relocated.

But she hadn't moved far from Shawlands Drive. It occurred to me that perhaps she was too close for any tolerable definition of comfort. I'd have the opportunity to ask her if this was the case, although only if I decided the question, and more importantly the answer, was pertinent. I was paying her a house call.

I stood outside her new residence and reached out to the front doorbell. I was expected and the door opened, doorbell slipping away from me before I had the chance to press. Ms Murray wasted no time in ushering me in.

We were in the hall. 'I find it difficult to sit,' she said. 'I'm up and down, up and down. Can I make you a cup of tea?'

'I...'

'Please, I'd be so grateful for something to do.'

'Okay, no sugar, just a tiny dash of milk please,' I said. 'Just enough to change the colour.'

'Great,' she said. 'Don't mind me, though, please sit.' We had reached the end of the hall and she motioned me towards the living room while she continued on to the kitchen.

It felt like I'd been on my feet for a week, and I shared none of Fiona Murray's reservations about being seated. I'd grown to enjoy the moment when you sit down on an unfamiliar chair, perhaps a little too carefully at first, certainly overcautious, leading with your hands, taking a moment to convince yourself that you're not going to fall through a trapdoor and, not before then, relaxing and leaning back into the cushion. But of course, I was easily impressed. I could make an adventure out of putting a slice of bread in the toaster. Still, the way the cushion gave way a little and then held fast was particularly satisfying. And even if it wasn't, practically speaking, I could always take this as a timely reminder to sit up straight.

She returned with a mug of tea, but only one, which was meant for me. 'Thanks,' I said as I took it from her. I looked down and registered a light brown swirl. 'Pretty spot on.'

She was standing next to me. Her face was puffy, scraped in places. She appraised the length of the coffee table set in front of me before looking at the chair further across from me, her body fidgeting, unsure what to do with her hands.

'Don't know when I'll be allowed back,' she said. 'They tell me because of the explosion there's an issue with the structure.'

I said, 'Ms Murray, can I call you Fiona? My name is Detective Sergeant Julie Spencer. Please, call me Julie.' I carefully, slowly, placed my mobile on the coffee table, my finger poised over the recorder function. 'You mind if I record the interview?'

'Yes, yes,' she said. 'The explosion? Those poor policemen. They were only doing their job. No one deserves that to happen to them.'

'Policeman and woman.'

This seemed enough to prompt her to walk past me, towards the vacant chair. 'Oh, you're right. I'm not thinking straight. I don't know how long it took for the police to arrive. Sometimes, when I think back, it was only a few minutes, other times I remember it as a lot longer. I have this constant headache. Can't close my eyes. I feel sick all the time. Really, I don't see what help I'll be.'

At this point, an older woman stuck her head around the door.

'It's okay, Mum,' Fiona said. 'We're just talking. No one wants anything.'

I directed a reassuring smile towards the head, only for it to have been hastily withdrawn already.

Still hesitant, still not seated, Fiona lifted the cushion from the chair and held it, pressed against the side of her face. 'I'm stuck with Mum. We don't get on. She's trying to be understanding, keeps her distance, and you know, it's just making things worse. I feel like I'm an intruder. The bastard has made me feel like I don't belong in my mother's house.'

It wasn't my place to pass comment. I tried not to think of my own mum. There would be time to reflect on this later. I would make the time.

'I'm sorry,' I said, 'but if I can take you back to that time, after WPC Cairns found you, you'll have heard the explosion?'

'The flat shook. It took out most of the front door. Plaster and dust, it fell from the ceiling. Shaken up, but...' A confused look crept across her face. She returned the cushion to its original position. She now sat on the chair. She was leaning forward, hands clasped. The chair didn't swallow her up whole, either. 'I was fine, really.'

'You spoke to the attacker previously. He broke into your flat.'

'Is he a terrorist? Peter McGarvey?'

'We're not calling him that. We don't believe so. You hear that name on the news? He's a suspect, yes, but that's all.'

'Was he in prison?'

'I need to be straight with you. Peter McGarvey was released two years ago under license, but that expired late last year. We have no idea of his movements since.'

'Oh. Shit. You think he'll come after me?' Even as she enunciated the words, her frame did not react in a corresponding way. Her lips said one thing, her body said something different. For someone who couldn't sit still, she hadn't flinched. She just sat where she was. For a few moments, we both did.

'We have no reason to believe that's the case,' I said. 'We're regularly patrolling the area. You should have a number you can ring, any time day or night, if you're worried anything is wrong. If you feel threatened in any way.'

'I try not to leave the house,' she said. 'There was another attack, another murder, nearby... There was a baby...'

'Child is alive and well,' I said. 'We can't say at this stage, first incident, second one, if there's a connection. Fiona, I can't stress enough, we're working night and day to keep everyone safe.'

'There was something about his voice,' she said. 'I'd need to hear it again, although I don't want to hear it again. Not in a million years.' Her hands formed each side of a cradle, like she was holding an imaginary mug in her hands. 'He handed me a scrap of paper with a circle drawn on it and straight lines coming out of it. It could have been a child's drawing of the sun. I didn't know what to do. How to react. "Can't you read?" he said to me.'

'He had this low voice, that and the mask, I had to strain to hear,' she said. 'But I didn't dare ask him to speak up. He had this bag. Ordinary shopping bag. He was rolling up his sleeve, jabbing with his knife up and down his arm. Then I was screaming and begging for my life.'

'After handing you the paper, did he say anything?'

'He asked me to scream,' she said, 'but before that...'

'Yes...?'

'Like I said, he asked me if I could read, if that wasn't messed up enough. He didn't seem interested in a reply. I think for a moment he forgot who I was, he forgot who *he* was. I think for a moment, I could have asked him to stop and he would have. There was something in his eyes. That's all there was to focus on, that and his mouth. *Where am I? Why am I here?*'—that's what his eyes were saying.'

As she made her statement, I could see the colour drain away from her face. It was as if she had just seen a ghost of her own making. A ghost that was trapped inside her head.

'He forgot who he was...'

I listened intently, feeling nothing but wave upon wave of sympathy for her. I would have said anything to make her feel better. 'We will catch him, I promise.'

I said the words, but just as importantly I believed them, too.

We both sat in silence, and then I reached down to the coffee table and ended the recording. 'Fiona, thank you so much for your time.'

And then part of me was preoccupied with more mundane matters. I was questioning my previous musings on the delights and possible pitfalls of sitting on a chair, where did that come from? When had I been co-opted into the tea and comfy chair brigade? When did I start becoming like him? Like the DI?

***

So, now I was in a bar, I plonked myself down on a barstool and hoped to dispel some inner demons.

My date turned up dressed in a mohair jumper over a black turtleneck top. I couldn't believe my own eyes. Such a combo could not possibly coexist. It just did not go. I grieved for the goat that lost its coat in order to make such a monstrosity possible. Perhaps it was the goat from up the side of the Alps.

He smiled and kept it there, fixed across his face for longer than could ever be considered natural. Eventually, it waned. 'Hi, Julie,' he said, and smiled again, confirming that it was no Robert-short-for-Bob smirk. Good start.

Good bleating start.

'Stevie,' I said, 'I can recommend the poison.'

'Excellent,' he said, executing more of a plop than a plonk down on the barstool next to me. He rubbed his hands with boyish enthusiasm. 'You on the bottles, I'll take a pint. You all right?'

'Not particularly.' I found myself smiling at this. Even though it was impossibly rude, and completely unforgivable, it was equally refreshing to take an axe to the chitchat and just put it out there from the off. Tell Stevie how I was really feeling. 'I'm surprised I'm even here to be honest. I'm tired, stressed, fed up, at the point of disrepair.'

'Disrepair?' he said. He seemed to shrug off my tirade (if that's what it was, at least that's what I thought it was) giving the impression he'd heard a lot worse. 'Sounds painful. You like this all the time?'

He took off the mohair, which went up and over, then wrapped it up into a ball of wiry tracks. He revealed, in its place, quite the buff torso. I could at least now look past the turtleneck, tight in all the right places, and call me genuinely surprised. A teensy bit impressed.

But the thing with surprise is that it's difficult to hide it. Or, should I say, with me, it's difficult to hide it. But if he saw it, picked up from me a giveaway widening of the eyes or a juddering flick of the hair, he gave no indication. Instead, he patted down his mohair on his lap, swung a little on his barstool, while stooping to take a couple of sips of his pint; the glass remaining steadfast on the bar. I had to admit it was a fascinating display. Just watching him in his natural environment.

'You a police detective?' he said.

'I am. It usually takes a little longer for this to come up in the conversation.' I could have added, in any ordinary conversation.

'It's just that...' He stopped and returned to his lager. This time he even lifted the glass.

'It's just that...?' I was good at that, repeating something someone says while shaping it as a question. If these dates had achieved anything, it was to point out, to me at least, some of my less than endearing habits, which wasn't ideal. But what were Scott of the Antarctic's last words despite facing impossible odds before sneaking out of his tent? Was it, *"I'll be back"*? Or was that Arnold Schwarzenegger? Anyway, the point was I was here, so let's just see the thing through.

'I would have expected more swearing,' he said.

'Come again?'

'You know, swearing, like a trooper. Or a police detective.'

'You mean like *fu...*'

I tried to position my mouth to say everyone's favourite four-letter special. If I got the mouth right, I reasoned, the vocal cords would surely follow. It was a simple thing. Not rocket science. *'Fyuh...'*

'Fyooo...'

The exertion continued. I tried to reel it in, only to experience utter helplessness as my mouth conspired to stretch away from the rest of my face.

Now it was his turn to watch on. He had both arms rested on the bar, head at an angle, banishing any initial bemusement at the spectacle for now, enjoying the show.

I contorted my mouth. I knotted my lips. '*Fu... Fu... Fu...*Fudge it.' I was breathless. This had almost broken me.

'Huh?' He smiled, and this one was as natural as they come. 'You want some fudge?'

I leaned forward and kissed him. After a few seconds of, presumably, frantic neural activity on his part, he kissed me back.

***

I was in my bedroom, my curtains twitching as I looked out onto my street. I'm not really sure why I did it. Force of habit I suppose. Sometimes—and at times like these especially—I longed for the simple life of finding lost cats and spying on the neighbours and that would be about it. Standing at the curtains, at least I had the decency to stoop down, not wanting to be seen. I was in a bra and not much else.

Stevie was laid out on his back in bed, on top of the covers, leaving absolutely nothing to the imagination. His hands, crossed, supported the back of his head. He seemed to be toying with saying something before choosing to keep his own counsel.

Clever boy. I crossed to the bed and lay down on top of him.

We kissed long and hard. I ate him up. His fingers at first fumbling, then more direct, once they found the latch of my bra.

We were so close, a hairpin away, when the image of Mrs Bartholomew popped into my head.

Yes, any euphoria carried over from yesterday was gone now. It had exhausted itself.

I rolled off and lay next to him. We were both catching our breath and I was grateful for the lack of dialogue between us, at least temporarily.

'What's up?' he said.

'I can't get the taste out of my mouth.'

'What?'

'There was this case in Milngavie,' I said. 'Surname began with a B.'

'Mrs B was taken, kidnapped, and her captor used a gardening tool to cut bits off her. Her fingers, her tongue. He'd then post them out to her husband in a Jiffy bag. We eventually found her, tracked her down. She had a sheet over her. When I tried to remove the sheet, I discovered it was stapled to her head. Her mouth was a puffy, purple mess. Her vital signs were fading when we found her. Maybe she was gone already. I tried to give her the kiss of life. Her mouth was fused shut; lips coated in dry blood. I couldn't get air into her lungs, but still I had to try.'

I could feel my body heat dip. The sweat that enveloped me now prickly against my skin.

'These kinds of things, they stay with you,' I said. 'And if the sensation, the taste, whatever the right word for it is, if it reminds me of anything, it's the desperation of it all, the pointlessness of everything. I didn't always feel like this. We're all struggling to breathe. That's key, I think. The worse it gets the more determined I am, the only thing I can make sense of is the will to go on.'

I glanced across and he was all flailing hands. He was putting on his jeans, practically stepping into them while heading out the bedroom door. A whirling dervish. A spinning top. A Tasmanian devil. The mohair-and-turtleneck combo was fast becoming something—in a few years' time, here's hoping, when I look back—that *might* have happened in my life.

Soft steps became heavy ones as he negotiated his feet in socks, then in shoes on the way downstairs. This was followed by the bang of the front door (handily for both of us, I'd left my key in the lock).

And I was left alone as naked as the day I was born, but absolutely none the wiser. And I looked down at the floor on his side of the bed. Not that he was here long enough for any of this to be *his* anything. And there on the floor was a pair of discarded underpants.

17.

3 Pubs

I took the stick with me, but did so this time for show. I liked the feel of it, the look of it, how my weight shifted alongside it. I liked the way it changed me; I was an outbreak of tripodal limbs. Of sixes and sevens, pistons and levers; how it signified the passing of time, an elephant in search of an elephant's graveyard. All I needed was a top hat and tails and I'd be perfect for the merry dance Bryce Coleman was leading me on.

He wanted me to start tearing things down and not to spare the horses. Although in my experience, the horses were the first to go. A case of equine collateral damage.

In any case, smashing things up, whatever the facet of organised crime, wasn't part of my makeup. Outside of traditional, methodical police work, I was of no mind to dismantle anything. What I really wanted was Peter McGarvey, the Balaclava Man, and Coleman wasn't backward in being forward about dangling him in front of me.

The prospect of Peter. For the moment, it felt like a roundabout with no end lay ahead of me. Where up was down, right was left, and front was anything but. But there were no other leads available to me even worth a mention. The fact was, Coleman was inside my head, and it wouldn't do any good to argue otherwise. I was committed, then, to follow this course of action in a resigned way. Resigned to follow this course of action in a committed way. Me and the stick.

From a practical sense, the stick offered a level of protection. Who would hit a man with a stick? Who would hit a man with a stick with a stick? It was all about common decency, itself wholly dependent on where you found yourself. In some places, common decency wasn't common at all.

And if this wasn't enough of an affectation for some types, I favoured holding the stick in my bandaged hand. The dressing hadn't been changed for a couple of days and, if I was honest, was looking quite grubby. I knew I'd need to up my game in this department. I would either need to start dressing my finger—what was left of my finger—every day, or select a darker colour of bandage, not white. It was tempting to steer clear of the white.

I was in familiar territory. I was back Southside. I'd grown accustomed to the smell of it. I was on a street with empty, windowless factories either side. It was like pieces of the building had been chipped away. The emotion of erosion. There was the taste of salt and grit in the air. No CCTV on the street. In the distance there was a mobile crane which betrayed no signs of movement, as if in suspended animation. I fought against the tide, pushing forward with the stick, willing my legs to follow in its slipstream.

All the while Bryce Coleman was yattering in my head. 'Looking in all the WRONG places. Everything is connected; INTERTWINED. Fucking MASKED men. Fucking Horses' HEADS. Something you can put your FINGER on. You want COLD hard facts, you go to the 3 Pubs. That's where the WRETCHED and sullied go to boast about their law breaking, their arm and leg breaking, all the lies and the occasional truth, while staring into each other's eyes searching for evidence of evil incarnate. The MAN in charge, he's elusive to the point they claim he doesn't exist, but I'll take you to him. Going on a PUB crawl from hell, I'll take you to the devil himself.'

I approached a building which could hold the potential for life, allegedly, but this wasn't clear from the outside. Facing me was a wooden exterior as black as the ace of spades. I stood in the midst of the 3 Pubs: the three worst pubs in Glasgow. They couldn't be anything else, purposefully so. The first of three pubs called—

'Jack in the Box,' I said. 'More commonly known as Jack's. Your plan is to set foot in there? That's crossing the line.'

'You either GROW a pair right now or come back

later once you've decided you've got the balls to grow some.'

Which was as nonsensical a statement as you were likely ever to hear (from inside your head), but I took the point even so.

It was perhaps inevitable that I found myself where I did. All paths in Scottish life led to a public house of some description, but it wasn't always a road well-travelled, not always without its perils. It could be a place where people met to whisper secrets, unwilling to accept the reality of the world around them unless experienced among and shared with the fellow clientele. Surrounded by those who, if pressed, shared the same worldview. A dull place shorn of natural light, of alcohol and background noise. Would my being there be accepted, add some colour, maybe even help legitimise things? *A pint glass runneth over*, if you will? Or would my presence bring it all crashing down—as Bryce Coleman might have hoped for? How I'd manage to achieve such an outcome, I still had no idea—with a twitch of the nose? There was only one way of finding out the answer.

As I pushed it open, the bulky wooden door seemed to burn the skin from my fingers. As I entered, I stepped among sawdust-covered bear traps which cluttered the wooden floor, threatening to crunch through cartilage. As I stood inside, my world came crashing down among the ceiling panels, raining down chunks of plasterboard and dust around my ears. Afraid to breathe or open my eyes in case the contamination sneaked in and turned the inside workings of my body against me, I could feel the bile rise into my throat, too toxic to consider swallowing it back down. I was a willing participant; the tempting of fate made my eyelids heavy. I not only crossed a line, but many of them, voluntarily breaking every one of my bones then resetting them along the way.

But none of this materialised. The fact was undeniable that I was still standing. I was in Jack's, Glasgow's equivalent of the Cantina bar from *Star Wars*. In the far corner, a two-piece band consisting of accordion player and flautist played the flight call of a migratory bird from Hell.

Surveying the belly of the beast, lined up either side were L-shaped snugs. In full view, punters sat with their heads bowed, pints in claw-like hands, while others were shooting up next to them. The central seating area consisted of round tables, like mighty Wagon Wheels (for want of a better biscuit). The males wore Led Zeppelin and AC/DC t-shirts. The females wore plain tops and skirts of muted colours. I was feeling a little overdressed, such as I was in a cashmere overcoat.

Everyone looked ten to fifteen years older than they actually were. They sat in groups, creating their own particular shrouds, their own veils of darkness, making a combined effort to expel the light. They would sometimes mutter at each other, but mostly to themselves, between a slug and snort of this, and a tab and puff of that. The smoking ban didn't appear to have reached Jack's. As Glaswegian '*a hive of scum and villainy*' as you could ever expect to see.

So far, the odd shifting of feet apart, there was nothing that I could call threatening behaviour. At least outwardly. Maybe the walking stick was having the desired effect, combined with a bandaged hand, making me appear harmless...

...As I actually was. And I could decide to wait out the time required for someone to eventually dislike my face enough to kick seven shades of *shit* out of me, or as way of alternative, do something as radical as order a—

'Diet Coke, please.'

On my walk to the bar, it occurred to me that the prospect of a diet coke was a distant one. Maybe at a stretch they'd have full fat Irn-Bru. But old habits, like Bruce Willis, die hard.

If you can picture in your head a man being dragged backwards through a hedge, then the barman resembled the hedge. He was wearing a skinny t-shirt cut off at the sleeves. Various track marks adorned his arms.

'One Diet Coke coming right up,' the barman said. He held up a chubby whisky glass to a wall dispenser. Brown liquid dribbled down into the glass. He turned, he grinned at me.

If this was a Diet Coke, it looked pretty flat to me.

The barman put the glass down on the bar. 'You want methadone with that?' He cleared his throat before swilling the resulting flotsam around his mouth. I could hear the sloshing. Maybe he had swallowed a fly?

The barman spat a dollop of chewy saliva into the glass. The spit stretched down from the top of the inside of the glass to the bottom, leaving a soapy trail. It resembled frogspawn in cloudy water.

I was conscious of those sitting in the L-shaped snugs and around the Wagon Wheels were now looking up, heads tilted, ear lobes flaring. Elsewhere, even the migratory call had stopped. The patrons of Jack's were finally paying attention.

I took the glass of grog-tinctured firewater to my lips and did what comes naturally in a dwelling such as this, despite my every neuron screaming at me to stop. I drank it from the side clear of the frogspawn trail, not that I suspected this would make a world of difference.

In my mouth, there was a warmth to the liquid which made me feel sick, followed by a burning sensation in my throat, which made me feel a different type of sick. A red dot popped up on the bridge of my nose, all the more to concentrate the pain, the separation of the skull like the parting of a hollow chocolate egg.

And then I swallowed hard, and kept on swallowing even after there was nothing left. And, mission accomplished, I brought the glass down with a thump on the bar.

'On the house,' the barman said, without a hint of emotion etched on his face. Which was disappointing, he could have been a tiny bit impressed.

All around, various heads returned to looking down and communing with the sawdust on the floor. They returned to their muted conversations. They returned to their chemical highs and lows. The music, if that's what it was, resumed.

The barman stuck a thumb, which was shoulder height, out to the side. It signalled a trajectory leading to an adjoining establishment. I had come this far. I was one of the rats so in awe of the Pied Piper. And the thumb was pointing the way. I was one of the children, also.

As way of verbal confirmation, the barman said, 'Take it next door, yeah?'

I shuffled my way to the door in question, and immediately noticed that dust had gathered on the door handle. My educated guess was that there wasn't much in the way of toing and froing from one level of the criminal underworld to the next. I was about to leave the hoi polloi to their devices—and vices—and enter a realm populated by a higher caste of criminality.

Educated guesses were what us detectives were all about.

I placed my hand on the handle, my frame leaning forward, only to encounter the jarring sensation typical of a locked door. Quickly, I gathered myself and knocked out a *ratatat*.

From the other side of the door, there was a rattling then the sliding of a lock. A moment later, the door swung open. There was no sign of who had done the rattling and sliding, but any kind of welcoming party could be deemed as not necessary, or expected, or indeed desirable. So, I walked through.

I was under no misapprehension, from one shark pool to the next, but with this one the clientele was better dressed. Each and every one of them wore a dark blue suit, the type of multipurpose garment appropriate for meting out a summary execution one day and attending the funeral of the victim the next. Dark blue informed very much the décor of the interior as well.

'Welcome to Mary's,' I said under my breath, my lips barely moving. So, in a way, I did have my welcoming party.

The area around the bar was as crowded as it was crooked. It was standing room only. Suited pub dwellers chatted, or were engaged in the illusion of chatting. Beyond the throng, in the corner, was by comparison an oasis of calm, consisting of dartboard and makeshift oche stitched into the carpet. In the middle of a game of darts were two more suited, crooked, standing, chatting pub dwellers.

One of the dart players had a blotchy, round, pummelled face not too unlike the pocked bullseye of an actual dartboard. He had the kind of face that, at the slightest hint of exasperation, could erupt into tides of molten lava. He was big-boned. And big everywhere else as well. I ID'd him as Danny 'Kebab Killer' McFadden.

Two of McFadden's darts already occupied the

treble 20 position, which meant he was one throw from attaining the highest dart score possible, which would lead to the rapturous refrain of bellicose angels that is 'One Hundred and Eighty!' One foot forward, elbow tensed, causing a rippling effect down one shoulder, McFadden wrapped thumb, forefinger and middle finger around his third dart. His leading hand swayed melodically, teasingly, grace under pressure, ready for the release.

Then, it all stopped. Danny twisted his head round, his eyes feasting on me. Then, beyond me. 'Who left the fucking door open?' he said. His gaze then left the doorway leading from Jack's to Mary's to recommence his glare at yours truly. His lips crawled into the creases around philtrum and labiomandibular fold, revealing an enraged set of yellowing teeth.

Like a flick of a switch, the other pub dwellers stopped their conversations. They held their drinks in mid-air and turned their heads en masse. Not just Danny, now everyone was looking at me. Me and the stick, we'd resumed the mantle of centre of attention. I took it upon myself to speak for the both of us.

Even so, I stood very still. I didn't need to move any. Everyone, it seemed, was coming to me.

I was quickly surrounded and tried not to be disorientated by the sheer number of suits. I had started counting them, only to give up once I reached the twenties. If I closed my eyes, the swish of flapping fabric could have been the swish of scimitars slicing through the air, which acted as the ideal reminder that there were men inside those suits. Men with blood on their hands already.

They might have been better dressed, but not better behaved. I watched helplessly as the space around me was gobbled up. This was followed with the crushing sense of inevitably that accompanies pushing and shoving. Jostled by weight of numbers, bumped along by a multitude of short, sharp punches, I was bounced like a rubber ball towards the corner with the dartboard. Somewhere along the way I lost my stick. I was surrounded by thieves after all. It didn't slow me down, compelled ever closer to those yellowing teeth and that 'Kebab Killer' stare.

'Put him over there,' Danny barked, wrist at a right angle, pointing a finger towards the dartboard proper.

I stumbled, but there was nowhere to fall. This brought about another flourish of jostling, a smattering of hurly-burly. So much for the man with a stick, who had now lost his stick. Hoping his stick would be handed in to lost-and-found.

A final tug of my coat instigated a thankless half-turn, and I was standing with the dartboard behind me. The back of my head was aware of it, the shafts of my hair caressing it. The darts previously on the board having been flattened by my trapezius muscle, now sent tumbling to the ground. This had me thinking, his chance of scoring 180 blown, what was Danny intending to do now with this third dart? My assailants tactically withdrew to either side of the throwing area. There stood as many as standing room allowed. Poised, looming over the oche was Danny, one remaining dart having sprouted on his hand like an additional appendage.

'You move from the board,' Danny said, 'even one bastard twitch, it'll be worse for you. A lot worse.'

I put both hands up in a placatory fashion and hoped this didn't qualify as a twitch in Danny's eyes. I said, 'Danny. Danny, isn't it?' Let's not do anything rash. I only want to ask a few questions.'

Another jab of the finger. At least I think it was his finger. 'I'm trying to be calm here,' he said. He looked pretty pissed off to me. 'But I'm having to think why I shouldn't stick this dart here straight up your urethra!'

Some of the heads in suits turned towards Danny with inquisitive glances.

'That's up your cock, you fucking Neanderthals!'

A now contemplative Danny, as he turned his attention back to me, tapped the dart on the palm of his hand. 'I've seen everything now. Is nothing fucking sacred these days? This boozer is out of bounds. You do not cross the line. And lo and behold, you've fucking crossed the line.' Danny's face was getting redder, and it was already scarlet to begin with. 'Either this or what's the alternative? When we need to relax an' unwind after punching some poor sod's teeth out for late payment of interest of £270.70, should we go to a copper's boozer instead? Should we?'

I had no answer to this, except the obvious one.

'You waltz in uninvited, giving us the eye,' he said, having overseen the transition from mildly contemplative to absolutely raging. 'Who do you think you are? Maybe I'll take out that eye, what do you think?'

I knew just what to think. Danny had an audience and it would be remiss on his part not to play to it. But the advent of the attention deficit in society in general was on the rise, and no more so than right now in Mary's. Danny went back to assuming a dart thrower's stance. I still had my arms in the air like I did not care (although I did, I very much did), my head remaining still and occluding the centre of the dartboard. The coup de grace, courtesy of Danny 'Kebab Killer' McFadden, wouldn't be long now. I was out of options but was thinking furiously. What else could I possibly do, where else did I have to go?

I felt a twitch from my bandaged hand, my brutalised finger. Not a twitch intended for Danny's radar. No, this twitch was meant for me. It could have been a beacon, a ray of light, a chance of getting out of the situation unscathed. Well, relatively unscathed. Such were the maddening thoughts that populated my head.

I slammed my hand against the wall behind me, replacing the twitch with shooting pain. My stump exploded, engorged by stabbing pulsating neuralgia. Images in my head, of spongy pus and dribbling infection flooding my shredded mind.

It was desperate. I was desperate. Maybe it would have been better just to take the dart, succumb to its sleek tungsten mercy, but I'd made my bed and now it was time to tuck myself in. Someone who was me but not me. It was all muscle memory, and the brain is the biggest muscle of all. It was all method acting, and I had my audience. I could prey on their gullibility; their longing to believe. I could make like it was shifting inside me, leaking out, a residue of him. A flavour of him.

A taster.

'I'm not that man anymore, Michael.'

My mind went hurtling back to that interrogation room in the Bar-L with Michael Doherty, and Bryce Coleman, and someone else. Someone I'm not. Not anymore. How many times do I have to keep saying this? Again and again, the exact same thing?

I don't need to be that man, Michael, to be that man. I just need to be true to myself.

'Well, well,' a voice growled. A voice as deep as the Kola Superdeep Borehole. Everyone with the capacity to look in Mary's was looking at me, so I must have been the source. 'Look at all you cunts. A real clusterfuck of cunts. And you, Kebab Killer, are the biggest cunt of all.'

'Yeah?' Danny said. Despite the memory muscle that was the bravado in his voice, this latest development had caught him off balance. He lowered his dart throwing arm.

'Fuck yeah,' the voice said.

I took a step to the side, turned my head round, gave the dartboard a look up and down. 'New board, eh? Very nice. Very plush. I have reason to believe this board is as hot as a baked potato cooked in the heart of a fucking volcano. Fallen off the back of a lorry; I want the name of that lorry.' I untwisted my head and directed my favourite death stare at the hoodlums lined up on either side of me in turn. 'Looking for volunteers. Any of you fandans want to help in my enquiries?'

'How about you, Kebab Killer? You anything to say? They dug up your sister yet?'

Danny McFadden said nothing, electing instead to stand grim faced. He held the dart now by the flight, point first.

'And Eddie MacBrayne, I see you.' I picked out a pub dweller from the crowd. 'How's the shin? I noticed the limp from earlier. You remember the time I kicked the fuck out of your leg? You've got so many metal pins in there, I hear you've developed a fucking phobia of magnets.'

Then another one. 'Matty Paatelainen, last time I had the privilege of your company, you shat yourself so much you lost two stone in body weight.'

'Pinky McPhee. You still have daddy issues? He's dead—been dead for ten fucking years—but still he climbs in next to you every night, eh? Have I gone too far?'

I turned and grabbed the dartboard and wrestled it off the wall. 'You're damaged goods the lot of you. You don't know how to remain silent. I'm not asking you to come quietly. I'll drag every one of you fuckers to hell if I have to.'

I switched the dartboard to one hand and threw it like a bulked-up Frisbee. It went spinning towards Danny on the oche.

It could have been sound and fury, with the emphasis on fury, but the intervention of gravity decreed that this should turn out to be a damp squib. The board landed, bouncing clear of his feet, at least forcing him to lift a leg. The Kebab Killer half-raised his hand towards the side of his head, as if in response to an insect buzzing in his ear. Now that I'd noticed, there *was* something the shape of an insect lodged in his ear.

Job done. Calm. Revert.

I took long breaths and I felt less hot. A gymnast was no longer exercising between my ears. I could relax my jaw. The tightness relented in my wrists and arms. Shooting pain was relegated to incessant throbbing, like the dripping of a tap, and I had endured a whole lot worse. 'I don't care about the dartboard,' I said, my voice having returned to the safe and sound of normal. 'You know why I'm here. Two police officers were murdered. Brutalised. Defiled. I'm not asking who did it, I'm not that naive to expect anyone here to be a grass, but I am asking why.'

In response, Danny adjusted his feet, tramping on the berthed dartboard as he did so. He turned and twisted his body, first aiming then throwing the dart towards the wall to his left-hand side. 'Treble twenty, ya bas'!' he said. 'On your own steam guv, fuck off while you can.'

The dart was embedded on the panelled outline of what could, now it was brought to my notice, have been a secret door.

I was of the mind, understandably, not to outstay my welcome. As I walked towards the door taking longer strides than usual, or was normally comfortable with, a hand jutted out from the suits handing me back my walking stick, which I accepted gratefully. It had been only minutes since our separation, but what minutes. It was like being reunited with an old friend. Stick in place, the pace dropped appropriately on my next step.

I stood in front of the secret door. It was like a perfectly rectangular block had been carved out of the wall. I had stood in front of many doors. It came with the territory. But what to do with this door in particular? The same as any, I decided. I knocked.

The door swung open. Soundlessly. Seamlessly. The only noise came from the scraping of a wooden stick on an otherwise unblemished and polished floor.

I walked into the third bar. What set it apart immediately was that this one was empty. It was as devoid of humanity as it was pristine. Modern fittings, it had the appearance more of a diner than a working man's bar: bright yellows, bright cream décor.

Behind the bar was a solitary man, diminutive, with a fluffy white beard. A pleasing change of pace to the psychos of before. He was drying a tulip-shaped pint glass with a chequered square towel. He wore a wireless headset.

'Take a pew, welcome to Albert's,' he said, motioning to one of the barstools the other side of the bar he worked behind. His voice was a little high-pitched, but in a way that demanded attention, which I guessed was the point.

'I'd rather stand.' I was momentarily distracted by the front pub window, specifically the view, now dominated by the mobile crane I'd spotted in the distance from before. I couldn't swear that this was the case, my bearings were shot to hell after the excitement of the previous two pubs; it did not appear to be manned, but the crane did look like it had moved. Back to the matter at hand, I returned to the barman and asked, 'Was I expected?'

'Were you expected?' he said. 'Yes.' He put down the glass in a way that suggested it had been swallowed up behind the bar. 'No.' He took off the headset, which he placed on the bar. 'Maybe.' He picked up a dimple pint glass and took the towel to it. 'Maybe not. I'll tell you something for nothing. Someone will have to pay for you being here. An example will have to be made. Broken bones. Permanent branding. It doesn't matter who, but if you have someone in mind I'm up for suggestions?'

'You're all OCG?'

'Yes, no ... OK I'll give you that one, but it's all context. Don't think in terms of organised crime, but of socialised crime. You rather we take over a nice residential pub instead? Hanging baskets and flowerpots? We need somewhere to go. You're only half a man, a shadow of another self, but you already know this.'

'I'm not sure what you mean,' I said. Was he trying to goad me? If by half a man he was referring to my monstrous other ego, then he needed to understand that time had gone. There was a line etched in the sand. Not a one-off as such, a second one after the incident in Barlinnie but, make no mistake, for want of a better description, I'd drawn inspiration from it one last time. I was done fooling everyone and the degree of contempt for those around me that this implied. I was bored of it. I'd used up the last of him. He was dead to me. Every drop, the well was officially dry.

'Everyone knows of the 3 Pubs,' I said. 'Everyone knows they should give it a body swerve if they can, but to claim it's a no-go area is bordering on preposterous. We wouldn't agree to such a thing.'

At this, his mouth began to form a smile before reeling it back in. He gave me a look at odds with the unthreatening white beard and I caught a glimpse of the apex predator lurking within. 'The murders of two police officers didn't happen too far from here, granted, and you're entitled to hit us hard as a result. I can't argue in principle, the war, as your superiors call it, against organised crime. We're all feeling the heat. We're all collateral damage. That's what happens when there is a war.'

'Under normal circumstances, I wouldn't have come here,' I conceded. He was taking me down too many rabbit holes and I needed to get him back on track.

I could have invoked the voice in my head that was Bryce Coleman (which had gone conspicuously silent) but I doubted even this would help hurry things along. 'But these aren't normal circumstances.'

'I agree.' He put down the beer glass and replaced it with a long wine glass. To achieve maximum coverage, he funnelled the towel inside the length of glass. 'You're in one piece. You and your decorative walking stick. You're in one piece so far.'

'Maybe,' I said. I raised my damaged hand. 'Maybe not. Roy Lichtenstein, I presume?'

There was a twinkle in his eyes. 'Does Roy Lichtenstein even exist? It's comforting in a sense to think that one person is in charge, making all the decisions. A strange comfort, but comfort none-theless. An order to the disorder. What do you think?'

'I can't cross the street without someone mentioning *Big Roy* under their breath. There are photos.'

'Old grainy photos of a young man, you mean, with optimism in his eyes? Looking forward to a future that might mean something to someone? Do I look like a *Big Roy* to you? Perhaps in terms of stature, you think, like Napoleon?'

'I have questions.'

'Peter McGarvey? The Balaclava Man? I expect you do.'

'Why?'

'I don't know why. I don't know how, to be frank, another person can kill another human in either cold or hot blood. I could try and explain why *I* would do it, hypothetically speaking, but as for anyone else I'm no cod psychiatrist. It's just that there are individuals out there who operate to a different moral code, not that I need to tell you that. And perhaps someone like me might have a use for someone like them.'

'So that's your *"Why"*. Is *"How"* not easier? It's not as if it's difficult. Prisons, police stations, their homes, their favourite boozer. If you're prepared to stretch, there's nothing outside your reach. Prisons, I think, are my favourite. You think about it, they're designed to not let people out; not to stop people from getting in. I can have my pick of the whole box.'

He began to dry a succession of Hi Ball glasses, lifting them then depositing them, one after the other, like a Las Vegas croupier dealing cards. 'It's like a dance between us and the authorities. We give them a bloody nose, they give us a bloody nose, that's the rules of engagement, the basis of all our understanding. I like to keep tabs on the crazies. Sometimes we need to use individuals like McGarvey to stir things up. Well, not *use*, strictly speaking, but nudge in the right direction and hope for chaos. Brace for chaos. In a war of attrition, McGarvey is as good a foot soldier as any.'

A brace of brandy glasses. 'It's about the build-up to the Climate Conference. We're all excited about it. The *Big Show* I hear you and your boys are calling it. What imagination! And in its aftermath even more so, the potential for massive rewards to be earned. You catch the bogeyman before the main event, the police will not only end the war, they will retreat into themselves, and create opportunities which might not arise otherwise.'

I'd heard enough. I started to walk away.

Roy Lichtenstein—because that's what he was—called after me, 'Something I said?'

I'd edged to the middle of the pub, the *tac-tac* of my stick leading the way. A movement, something metal, caught my eye. From outside, I could swear just there that the crane had moved. 'I'll be back with a warrant,' I said. 'You're making a fool out of me. What you're saying is not possible. Not a word of it. There is no *dance*, there is no *understanding*.'

'You don't like the answers.' There seemed to be the hint of genuine sadness in Roy Lichtenstein's voice. 'How about this one? When you open your eyes, look up. Let your eyes take you to him.'

I put up a hand and waved goodbye. I didn't intend this to be ironic, but if that's how he took it then fair enough. In my wake, a shape was looming. The front window took on a life of its own.

There was a brutal concertina of noise as the façade of the pub disintegrated around me. There was an earth-shuddering clatter. A crashing. A booming. Glass like slanted rain.

The hook of the crane, having made light work of the pub, hurtled through, swinging low. I gripped onto my stick, which I held with both hands in front of me, effectively dividing me in two.

I leaned back, which was all the momentum of the situation allowed me.

Nothing to do otherwise, as the monster hook knocked me clean off my feet.

I lay dazed on the pub floor, slam dunked, arms sprawled out to either side. Stick wasn't far from my side, though.

I wasn't aware of any bleeding, but the whole of my body was numb in any case. My sagging eyelids could just make out the blur of the hook swinging above me, moving to and fro in imperceptibly smaller arcs, creaking while it did so, taking an eternity to come to a dead stop. It might have been the hook that was creaking, but it might have been me also.

On the periphery of my vision was a hunched shape on its tiptoes, looking very much like a prancing *Looney Tunes* villain, but I was hallucinating surely. Next thing I was aware, Roy Lichtenstein was bent over, whispering in my ear. He was so close, his beard tickled my earlobe, which was excruciating, an itch I could not scratch. A worse feeling than even being hit by a crane.

'Now where were we?' he whispered. 'It's my business to know everything.'

I was feeling very sleepy. The hush of his words only helping to send me on my way.

Hands strategically placed on my side and back, he lifted me. Before I knew it, I was sitting up. It knocked the stuffing out of me, or at least what stuffing I had left. I couldn't breathe. I clutched my chest. He kept his hands there so he could support me, although the idea of support was the last thing on my mind.

'You think your fucking kind can just waltz in here and there will be no consequences?' he said, snarling, hushed voice no more, not even the sense of it. 'I'm going to tear all three of these buildings down and we'll take on other establishments elsewhere. Somewhere nicer, I haven't decided. Maybe there *will* be hanging plants this time. Demolition is already in progress, as I am sure you are aware.'

He withdrew the support of his hands. 'Best vacate the premises,' he said.

I fell back onto my back with an almighty thud. Such was the force of habit, it hollowed me out. I winced in pain, but it was a temporary pain. Not built to last. I was fading into unconsciousness.

I was vaguely aware of Roy Lichtenstein getting on his feet. And I'd learned over the years that even a vague awareness was something worth holding on to. As long as you could. Roy Lichtenstein was walking in a normal manner this time, maybe the odd skip to his step as he approached the hook. The hook was now stationary and awaiting further orders. Big Roy reached out to it.

'We are all in the gutter but some of us are looking at the stars,' I think he said, but I could have imagined it. I could have equally imagined him stroking the hook as well. 'I'm feeling generous. Now listen, the Thirtieth Floor. Number 15. You'll know him by the Pigface.'

Then, I was no use to anybody, including and especially myself. I was out cold.

I'd blocked him out. I'd jammed the transmission. All my adult life I'd blocked out many things, just like my childhood. I'd strangled that one to death.

I wasn't interested in something, whatever the information, which did not help me, or inform me, or warn me. Always face forward, never looking back. At least that far back.

And yet, I was a mess of contradiction. I thought about little besides in hospital. I had exhausted everything else when all I had was time to think and overthink. How in foster care I'd tried on various masks, trying to decide which one suited me best. Taking a paper plate and drawing an angry face on it, a happy face, a serious face, a silly face. And holding that face up to cover my face, a flotilla of discarded plates piling up around my feet.

And now, there was the emergence of Peter McGarvey, making everything feel more and less important, like every dream I ever had was now connected to him. Even the dreams I did not want anymore. A set of eyes and mouth. A balaclava. A paper plate.

***

Pain. I had grown so much more accustomed to it, it didn't matter much what or where. Or how. I had regained consciousness, still groggy, finding each time I opened my eyes more of a surprise than the last. I woke lying on a dust sheet, which had obviously been put there like I had been put there—which was Big Roy's doing, it must have been—on top of a mountain of rubble. My walking stick was tucked in beside me, but this was the only thing still intact. And I included myself in that. The 3 Pubs no longer existed, reduced to their constituent parts.

I lifted my head, supported by my elbows, and I could feel the uneven expanse spreading under me. I could feel various fragments of debris sticking out and prodding and jagging into me. Roy Lichtenstein was gone. The nefarious patrons of Mary's and Jack's all gone. The mobile crane was gone.

'Climate change is not a lie, please don't let our planet die!'

In place of the crane on the street was a motley crew of brightly dressed protestors holding placards, carrying messages on the lines of 'Act Now' and 'Climate Emergency'. The clock was ticking with the Big Show due at the end of the year. And, depending on who you talked to, the end of the year was still some time away, or it was imminent. Time was no longer linear. For me it had lost the property a long time ago (whatever that phrase now meant). The city and the planet were following suit.

Seriously, though, they had demolished the 3 Pubs? Scorched earth?

Could I think of a more perverse overreaction to my trespassing on their precious establishments? There must have been another reason for it. Otherwise, had the world had gone mad? Madder than me? *Badder* than me?

'Now listen...'

I looked past my wracked and ruined body. I looked past the protesting peacocks. I looked up. Dominating the skyline was the Victoria Flats. It had always been there. It was a constant, a derelict behemoth. It was there at Shawlands Drive and Cathcart Road and now in the flattened residue that used to be the 3 Pubs.

'...the Thirtieth Floor. Number 15.'

Something was vibrating in my coat pocket. Miraculously, my phone was still in working order. Equally miraculously, someone had chosen to phone me. I had a vague recollection of last using my phone to book an appointment at the barbers. That and the fact I only accepted calls from numbers I did not recognise.

Case in point, DS Spencer called earlier. I ignored it. I let it go to voicemail. No sign of a wet sink to persuade me to reconsider. There may very well have been several out of sight, buried under the rubble. I wasn't answering any physiotherapist's calls either.

I scooped out the device, registering that the number on the screen was indeed a mystery to me. Having utilised a sliding finger, I took a moment trying to locate the speaker option on the phone, but this had proved to be a blind spot previously. I only seemed to select speaker when I didn't actually want it. An additional moment later, I was already lifting the phone up to my ear.

'Hullo,' I croaked.

'Fisher?'

'Speaking.'

'Hammond. You asked me to call. The flower...'

'Excuse me?'

'The flower submitted for analysis. You asked that I keep you updated.'

'Yes, that sounds right, thanks.'

'Afraid it doesn't look like it's going to lead anywhere. It's Carpobrotus. Rare for this part of the world. The name is derived from the Ancient Greek for fruit, *karpos*, and edible, *brotos*. More commonly known as Pigface...'

'Pigface,' I repeated, I carefully enunciated, taking more care than was necessary over the utterance of one word, two syllables. I began to see things clearly now. A way to put the universe back in the correct order. To slot it into its rightful place. Sometimes you can have everything, and all from a single flower.

'...Or edible fruit,' Hammond said. 'Someone will send out a written report for the end of the week. You okay, Fisher? You sound a tad woozy.'

'Just woken up.'

'Oh, on a more positive note, the note left at Shawlands Drive, the Post-it left at Cathcart Road, we're reasonably certain they were written by the same hand.'

'How certain?'

'I'd say 95%.'

'Thank you,' I said.

The line went silent. Dead.

I'd been dead before so I knew I was close to death, but I wasn't there yet. I could tell the difference.

I took a moment to send a text, which simply read 'Peter McGarvey', before switching off the phone entirely. Where I was headed, there would be no more interruptions.

And it was time to get moving. I considered rolling off the dust sheet and down demolition mountain. I'd keep rolling across the street before I'd even consider the arduous process, the contracting of muscles and hauling of bones, of getting to my feet. The moment passed though, making way for the good sense to bite my lower lip and be brave, and not put off the inevitable.

18.

Date No. 4

I was full time on the case, but this didn't stop all the other little jobs and assignments and errands piling up as well. The ones I'm expected to fit in somehow. I reasoned I could get by with a minimum of five hours of sleep before being reduced to a gibbering wreck. FYI, that's five hours per day, not per week. Maybe allocating an additional hour here and there, if not to ensure the body's continued health then, you'd have to hope, its survival. There just wasn't enough time. There just weren't enough hours in the day.

Case in point, I received by text a request to oversee the incineration of a seized drugs haul later that morning. A drugs haul that had absolutely nothing to do with me. Apparently, none of the actual arresting officers were available and a representative from Police Scotland was required to attend. Any representative, apparently; to cross the i's and dot the t's. No acknowledgement of the short notice. Another job, assignment, errand—take your pick I don't know—to add to the list.

I considered phoning the office, however fleetingly. Not sure what they'd say that I didn't know already. They almost certainly wouldn't have made a decision for me, outside a gentle reminder to GET IT ALL DONE. I thought about phoning the DI. He'd not reported in for a couple of days, as is his want. As is his sweet, unsullied, ruddy annoying M.O. Too many times it was left to me to chase him up. He only got in touch when he needed something himself. To be blunt, the more I attempted to interact with him, the more distant he seemed to get. Which said to me, what exactly?

Too much was happening around me, which directly involved me. Outside of work, I normally sought out the quiet life. A steady existence. No alarms and no surprises. And now, suddenly, all hell was breaking loose. I thought I could plunge into the balaclava case and the dating game and somehow combine the two while keeping both apart. But now it was like everything was getting out of hand. I was still grieving for my mum. Nothing on the horizon to suggest that this state of affairs might change any time soon. Somehow mixed in with this, never far, like a bad smell, was the DI. It was like I was waiting for him to trip up, make a mistake and reveal another side to him. I hated how he got away with everything and I got away with nothing. I wanted to see him incriminated, implicated, brought to task. And I wanted to save him. In some ways, he was a convenient diversion, an inconvenient truth. It just felt like I first needed him to get his life sorted out before I could then do the same with mine.

'JS, JS,' I muttered to myself. It wasn't enough to think the words, I needed to vocalise them. I was claustrophobic inside my own skin. 'You need to clear your head.'

Maybe I would attend the incineration after all. Maybe having a break from absolutely everything else might do me good for a little while. Maybe I could kill two birds with one stone, and then maybe dispose of the bodies.

***

I drove on the M8, taking the middle lane right up to the turnoff, leading to the waste incinerators at Osprey House. Having arrived, I needed to navigate a security tunnel to the outdoor incinerator units, but it helped that I was expected. I had a small plastic bag with me, which passed through the X-Ray machine in situ without incident.

The incinerator units weren't quite the great outdoors, but looking up, you could see that Osprey House was surprisingly close to Glasgow Airport. I stood gazing at the planes dominating the skyline, coming and going, and I forgot myself for a few glorious moments.

A voice called out. 'You from the cop shop?'

I turned to see a man in his thirties clad in oversized sterilised blue rubbers. Every time he moved, the material made a slapping noise, like plastic sheeting thrashing in high winds.

'I am, for my sins,' I said, 'but don't hold that against me, I'm basically a good person at heart.'

'Okay, that's good to know,' he said before swinging his arms out either side, bent at the elbows like wings. He was either impersonating a bear or taking a moment to stretch his chest and back muscles. 'I'm Agent Beale.'

'Not Special Agent Beale?'

'I'm in waste management, not the FBI, Ma'am.'

I was resigned to the fact that bad patter, from men primarily, had a habit of following me around. I was truly cursed. The shape of his body language seemed to suggest he expected me to say something, but right at that moment I had nothing to say.

'I have the paperwork,' he said eventually, having realised that waiting any longer wouldn't bring a response any closer. 'All present and correct. Triple checked on the scales. I can even throw in a song and dance number. *Knees Up Mother Brown* anyone?'

Oh, dear God, make it stop. Across from me, across from both of us, were hundreds of vacuum-packed bags on a tarpaulin sheet in a pile the size of a small hill.

'Oh, yeah,' he said, following my gaze. He looked like a little lost boy. I liked that look. 'Now that's about a quarter of a million Etizolam tablets, give or take,' he said. 'Seized from the Victoria Flats. Street value of 100 grand, give or take.'

'Victoria Flats?' My ears pricked up at this. 'Isn't that abandoned? Up for demolition?'

'Yes, no, yes,' Agent Beale said. He took a deep breath. 'The bottom floors are hoaching with criminal activity. Wouldn't say onsite security is particularly onsite or secure. The odd police raid clears them out, but they're back before you know it. But you're correct, Ma'am, the Flats are coming down. Next couple of weeks. Whoomph.'

'Not taken too close an interest,' I said. I'd never checked, never enquired. I just assumed the Flats were empty and unloved. To be fair, no one around me had set me right, at least up until now. Not that, thinking about it, I would have been too fussed whether there were squatters or not. It was all about the building and the fact it was coming down. If the DI was here, I could reassure him again; don't be afraid of the Big Bad Flats. 'I've been busy.'

I thought the Flats repelled him, but how many times had the DI confounded expectations and defied logic—at least my expectations—at least my logic. A year ago, he should have shared the same fate as Bryce Coleman. Not Lazarus, not anything. He should never have survived the fall.

And I was back there, when he wasn't there. I was climbing flights of stairs. Reaching the top of a five-storey building, scene of a crime both frightening and bewildering. When I peered over, I thought how far down it was—imagining how it would feel—to put myself in his place. I was curious, furious; a maddening curiosity, an enduring fury. Falling, trying to suck in air, flailing limbs, searching in vain for solid ground, until it was too late. Life flashing in front of you, me, him, edited and pared down, merged and overlapping, but all the same destined for the cutting room floor.

How it would feel to be him. But I had no answers. I was bereft of understanding. Not yet at any rate, but God forgive me, I had hope.

'Let the burning begin!'

So went the clarion call which brought me back to the here and now. Agent Beale was already shovelling the first batch of drugs to the ovens.

I said, 'Just you and a quarter million pills?'

'Normally Agent Parker is around to give me a hand, but he's off to Benidorm for the week,' he said. 'Not a worry, I'm surprisingly nimble on my feet.'

I held up my plastic bag. 'You couldn't throw this on the fire as well?'

He finished his first run before taking the plastic bag from me. 'Can I take a peek?' Not waiting for an answer (he'd learned his lesson from before), in the background several thousand tiny capsules popping in the heat, he pinched both sides and opened the bag wide and looked directly down.

Instantly he looked back up. 'A pair of underpants?' he said. He looked back down again and gave the bag a shake. All the while his eyes were widening. 'And what's that next to it?'

'An oven glove,' I said, before quickly adding, 'I needed something to pick up the pants with.'

He thought about it. He rolled his eyes clockwise then anticlockwise. 'Sure,' he said. 'No skin off my nose, if you agree to buy me a pint sometime.'

Fresh, I thought. Fresher at any rate than those undies in the bag. I thought about it but resisted the temptation to follow suit and roll my eyes as well.

'OK, Agent Beale,' I said. 'You've got yourself a deal.'

19.

Will the Real Pigface Please Stand Up?

I had a tin of peach slices today. South African in origin, or so the label on the tin said, and I had no reason not to believe it. The sweetness of the juice caused the receptors in my brain to spike, which was in sharp contrast to the dullness which otherwise followed me around in my derelict flat stuck up in the clouds. The rumbling grey clouds.

I had boarded up the windows with a blood-stained hammer. Other than this, I had grown sedentary. Even the thought of movement made me dizzy and want to vomit. I had inadvertently murdered three, perhaps four souls, and for what? What had I learned?

I didn't have to kill them for them to no longer exist. No longer *longer* exist.

The outside world had nothing for me. It had no answers.

All death was incidental, a means to an end, the pursuit of inner truth. I thought these acts would bring about a change inside of me. Back in prison, Horse Peter had said as much to me. Had promised as much.

I'd wanted to find my true face, only to discover that I had discovered it already. Before the broken bodies, before the pig mask, I'd been happy with my balaclava.

There was a knock on the door. The type of knock that wasn't for relenting any time soon. I wanted one hand free so, faced with a choice, gun or machete, I retrieved the revolver from the bottom of the cupboard. I had decided to make a last stand in this flat. In the Flats. These four walls made for an approximate of the world; they had served me well.

I answered the door, opening it only so wide, bringing matters to a halt mid-creak. I kept the gun out of sight. The man standing directly outside had short hair, ruffled, stylistically so. In his 40s perhaps, but his eyes were older. He wore a long coat. He held up an open plastic wallet with what might have been ID, but the polythene was too shiny for me to properly make anything out. It didn't matter because he recognised me instantly. He saw past the layers. His lips began to move—and I knew I'd have to act now or risk falling under his spell.

My body tensed before pushing the door fully open and swinging my previously hidden arm into full view.

He recognised what I planned to do, hips twisting, his leading foot already inside the door. He reached out to me with both hands in an attempt to limit my movement.

I squeezed the trigger. We were in such close proximity to each other. I felt the effect of the gunshot, ringing in my ears, pushing me back. The noise showed no signs of abating. I watched the man in front of me collapse like a deck chair.

***

This is what I meant to say.

I meant to say, 'Peter...'

'...Roy Lich...'

'...sent me...'

'...Peter.'

Instead, there was an explosion in my chest, and words lost all meaning. I'd fallen off the edge before, but never like this. There was a hole in me the size of the world. I'd experienced losing a part of me before, but never *anything* like this.

The bullet ripped a chunk out of me, bringing forth a crimson flurry, fury, like a backfiring car exhaust. Like a hole puncher through paper. And I had no choice but to follow its lead. In pursuit of a speeding bullet, I was tumbling into oblivion.

I drifted back to the cliff face that was my childhood. I was hanging from the precipice. Ferried from one family to another. Not the victim of bad choices necessarily, but of bad decisions definitely. It was not as if anyone was cruel to me, or unkind. Unless you considered neglect an unkindness.

One family had a son not much older than me. I was fascinated by him, I followed him around. I was a constant.

I rarely interacted with him, though. It was enough to be in his slipstream. I wasn't long with the family, but to be taken from this boy, the feeling of separation that stayed with me, tore away at me, did so for such a long time. I grieved for the loss of that boy in my life. I grieved for no longer being in his company as he scribbled out characters from *Star Wars* on a notebook, or formed shapes out of Lego bricks, or kicked a ball against a wall.

I'd never talked about my childhood to Dr Dawn. I wouldn't have known what to say or where to start.

'*Start at the beginning,*' she'd say.

But there was no beginning to childhood—there *was* only childhood. You either had one or you didn't.

How I revelled in the fact the boy would find a quiet place to eat a chocolate biscuit. (If I was lucky enough, I'd have a custard cream.) I continued to grieve for a time, even after I could no longer remember the boy's name. I think I must have known it once. Was it Harry, Roy, James, David, Luke...?

He could have been called Peter...

He could have been called the Balaclava Kid...

He could have been called Pigface...

Smelling of mother bacon...

Little piggy Pigkid...

I could have drawn his face on a paper plate...

***

I was back. I had returned to the land of the living. Allegedly.

I had lost consciousness for a short while there, and it had been a sufficient period of time for me to find myself sitting in a pool of my own blood. There was a hole in my chest and back. Along the way the bullet had bounced off my chest bone. It tore through me having hit no vital organs. Everything was relative. It was lucky.

My old friend was back, more overwhelming and overbearing than ever, and always to outstay its welcome. Pain. I could just about cope with it, so long as I stayed perfectly still. If I moved, even thought about moving, the threshold was lowered to a point beyond endurance.

I was inside Flat Number 15 on the Thirtieth Floor, with what remained of my back up against the wall. I placed my hand on my chest, a futile gesture. I was just glad to be alive.

Sticky all over. The hole in my back was in that place where, no matter how much you tried to adjust and stretch, it was impossible to reach.

Peter must have carried me in and put me down here, that would be the logical conclusion. I tried to gather my bearings all in the one place, but what more was there to know?

All the while, he stood several feet from me, silent,

wearing a ski mask, which had the appearance of being unnaturally filled out. The rubber neck was a giveaway.

There were so many bits of paper scattered around, it could have passed for a ticker tape welcome.

'You're indestructible,' he said, his voice horribly muffled, achingly so.

'More lives than a cat burglar,' I said, my voice amounting to little more than a hiss. The air released from a punctured tyre. Balancing minimal effort against the exertion of air. I was just the right side of audible. It helped, at least in this respect, by the fact my surroundings were still, irreproachable; as silent as the grave.

'Ah used to believe this was mah true skin,' he said.

He began to unpeel the balaclava, taking an inordinate time to do so, taking care not to disturb what lay underneath. I thought it would serve him right if I passed out before he was finished. Finally, so revealed, a man in a pig mask. Whatever emotions were flooding my system at that point, along with the endomorphins, surprise was not one of them.

'Then ah fought this might be mah true skin,' he said. 'And now...'

It was impossible to read his features behind the mask, but his body language could have suggested despair and disappointment. Resignation? I hoped for his sake, for all of our sakes, Peter McGarvey had reached the end of a rocky, turbulent, violent road.

Sewn on to the front of the mask, there were

shrivelled translucent, wafer-shaped patches. At the back of the mask, which I could make out thanks to his regular twitching of the head, like he was a third man, third pig, third budgerigar, was a large, shredded, deep, purple-tinged hole. The result of wear and tear. The type of wear and tear, I could only surmise, caused by the previous wearer—Samuel Cowan of Cathcart Road, however temporary at the time the arrangement between Cowan and mask was—being clubbed to death.

The firearm was still in McGarvey's hands. He held the gun limply, but for me, there was only cold comfort to be gleaned from such a display of listlessness. I had to keep him talking, keep him engaged, and buy myself some time. Enough time to finish the job I had started, which at that moment, to all intents and purposes, was to slowly bleed to death.

I had to choose my words wisely or I was a dead man, plain and simple. Namechecking Roy Lichtenstein wouldn't cut it. I needed to raise the stakes higher than that. 'I knew Horse Peter,' I said.

There was no reaction to this, none that I could see. Which was fine in my book. No reaction is better than a negative one.

'I was there at the start,' I prodded further. 'I was at the stables in Tannoch. I found the horse he killed and skinned.'

He held up his hand, close to his mask, and kept it there. There was no further movement.

'Not many people know about that,' I continued.

'That's not how he got his name, and he was never charged. After the carnage he perpetrated later in Glasgow underground, the act paled in comparison. It fell through the cracks.'

'You were there...?' he said. 'Mah name is Peter, too.'

'I know.'

'Fallen frough the cracks, you say? That describes me rotting in prison, messed up in the head. Empty. But Peter showed me ah could be somefing more. That ah could carry on the work. He taught me before you do somefing, you imagine it in your head and that's how it happens, like they are both the same. The two police officers—and then that young family—ah imagined it all beforehand and that's how it happened. And ah hid a baby in a bush, so it wouldn't be a part of it.'

'He told me to take the face of what ah feared most and so conquer mah fear. *Like he did.* From a young boy, he was terrified of horses you see. To then take that face as mah own face. *Like he did.* And to pass that face on, and so make it permanent. Make it forever. *Like he did wif me.*

'And now...?' I said.

'And now...' He followed my pause, which had itself followed his pause from earlier. 'Ah fought ah would be complete, but ah feel disenfranchised, dis-embodied. Like mah hand doesn't belong to mah arm. Like mah head doesn't stretch all the way around mah skull.' His mask took a breath. In and out it went. 'Like ah'm some alien who doesn't understand what it is to be human, and is misunderstood in return. Ah fink there are limits to mah imagination and time is running out.'

'You're in a bit of a muddle,' I said.

'Ah'm in a muddle?' he said. 'You should take a look at yourself.'

I had to give him that. I wondered for a moment where all this blood was coming from. I said, 'Do you remember the day Horse Peter died?'

'Ah was there at the end,' he said. 'Maybe he slipped in the shower, maybe he was pushed. Ah have no way of knowing and it does not matter anyway. There are worse ways of dying in the Bar-L. There are worse ways of dying anywhere.'

He sat back, perhaps on a table or something, perhaps he was floating in the air. He lifted his gun and aimed it once more my way. He had regained a sense of purpose that had been otherwise lacking moments before. He became the creature we both knew he was. Something capable of cold-blooded murder.

Someone like me—but that wasn't me—that was never me.

'Ah watched you as you drifted into unconsciousness,' he said. 'You were in shock. Ah watched the colour drain from your face, and then you opened your eyes.'

'Go ahead, do what you have to do,' I said. On balance, an acceptance of oblivion as opposed to some random pleading for my life. At this point, my life probably meant as much to me as it did him. 'Trust me,

I'm tired. I'm tired of change. You ask me, change is grossly overrated.'

'Don't say that.' Despite the conciliatory tone in his voice, his arm remained rigid; the gun remained pointed. 'Everyfing matters, or what's left? The humdrum; the terrible, belittling humdrum.'

'Just do it,' I said. I grimaced. It was an involuntary grimace. I couldn't stop grimacing if I tried. None of this felt like a reprieve. I was flitting between double vision and not seeing at all. Soaked in my own blood. I wanted to shout, scream for help, but a paralytic combination of loathing and pain had me in its grip. Loathing, self-loathing. I wondered if Bryce Coleman had already poured out a glass of whisky in anticipation.

'Laughing?' he said. 'Why are you laughing?'

I wasn't aware I was laughing, not until *Pig Peter* brought it to my attention. It was useless. It was insane. A form of suicide. With every contraction of the respiratory system, with every heave, I was aware of the blood spurting out of me.

'My finger no longer hurts,' I said, amazed that I had enough blood pumping inside of me to still articulate. I still had a few moments more. 'My finger that is no longer there. My phantom finger. Sometimes I imagine it's still there and that it's somehow grown back. Perhaps it's a memory of when I did have it, before it was snipped off by a pair of heavy-duty secateurs. I've come to attach so much importance to it. Something that is no longer there. It doesn't prevent me from doing anything. It's not a disability. I can write, drive a car, switch on the remote. But it's so much more important to me. It holds a greater value than you could ever know, now that it no longer exists.'

'That's the reason I'm laughing,' I continued, unsure if I'd survive another bout. Unsure if I'd really want to. 'It no longer hurts, my phantom finger, but my arms, my legs, my head, now everything else does.'

All my protestations of before now up in smoke. Up in vapours. What I was no longer up for was the fight. The loss of too much blood for it to matter anymore. I couldn't control any of this. There was only one thing, if I was lucky, I was ever in control of.

Not someone, something. Turning into something else. I was snarling now. My mouth an open wound, just like the rest of me. My jaw started to jut in and out involuntarily. Like I was a rabid dog, starved for days, for a taste for flesh, any kind of flesh.

In the mix, all of a sudden, in the death throes, there was a strange craving. A desire so great to reach out and grab this man in a ridiculous mask and break every moveable part in his body.

'You want to change, just do it,' I said. My left hand drifted away from me; in front of me.

'I'm sure you'll find something kicking about that's up for the job,' I said, my heart pumping, doing the best with what it had at its disposal.

The roar of blood in my ears. How did it get there? There was more meat on the bones than I remembered. What bones I had left.

'Why leave it at one,' I said, my voice as deep as the earth's core. 'And tell me what you see.'

'Just do it,' I said, and grimaced some more.

20.

The Flats

I looked up and, not for the first time, all I could see was the Flats. A giant vertical slab, a monster monolith, all thirty storeys of it. I was close enough to it, when I looked up, that I could not see the sky.

I knew it sounded daft to even think it; there it was, the feeling of the Flats following me around. As rooted to the spot as it was. But it was a very large spot. And now I was so close, I couldn't lie, the idea gripped me that I'd look up and someone from on high would be looking back down.

Officially, the last of the occupants shipped out and rehoused months ago. The building was empty. That was up until Agent Beale dissuaded me of the notion. It turned out Old Hughie—with his hidden banana and the lengths he was willing to go to illegally source a fish supper—was not the last resident of Victoria Flats after all.

Call it curiosity—a maddening curiosity—but I wanted to pop in. I wanted to see for myself how easy it would be to sneak into the Flats and gain access.

I decided against phoning it in. I had no intention of staying long. Not much more than poke my head in. Before anyone knew it, I'd be back out again.

I advanced and the shadow cast by the structure fell on the terrain around me, swallowing me whole. I was in its thrall, the beating of a giant's wings, more than an idea, a compulsion, this time making me look up, my neck craning to the point it didn't feel like it belonged anymore. I saw a flock of birds disperse from the very top of the building. I was too far down, too rooted to the ground, to discern what had spooked them.

The cause of the commotion might have come down to the actions of a security guard, except for the fact, so I'd subsequently discovered, the contract between Glasgow Council and the security firm G4 had never been signed. *An administration oversight,* I hear you cry. Or someone cry, if there was anyone around to do so, that is. *Or something more underhand?* I'd made some enquiries. A councillor had issued a complaint. An internal investigation was ongoing. Check in again, in about a hundred years.

Not a dickie bird, except for the real actual birds. They were starlings maybe. Little blobs of soot grey definitely.

I tried the main door.

There was a little give, but it was standing firm. I

pushed some more. From the other side I heard a chain rattle.

'Now, JS,' I said, 'you don't expect it to be *that* easy?' Part of me was disappointed I couldn't just waltz through the door, while acknowledging the other part of me that would have been just as disappointed if it were that simple.

I began the walk around the perimeter of the block, looking for signs of disturbance. Looking for a rabbit hole. I found an upturned plastic container handily positioned below a smashed window. I hadn't exactly struck gold, but it would have to do. Shattered glass adorned the general vicinity like spiteful confetti. The container itself was cracked. There was a flap of plastic where someone had partially put their foot through it. The box was a good size, true, but was it still sufficiently intact? Would it take my weight? Oh, the drama. Only one way of finding out.

I lifted myself up from the launching pad of the container and, ever mindful of where I was putting my hands, climbed tentatively enough through the window. Shards of glass, stubbornly attached to the frame, pierced various parts of me, slashing at my coat and jeans. Some even scratching the skin, maybe even drawing blood, but I wasn't of a mind to check. I was committed, no point going back now, the shards would soon be behind me.

I dropped down into an empty room. There was a lone poster of Taylor Swift on one of the walls. One of the corners was noticeably ripped, but otherwise,

I thought, she was looking remarkably intact, was Taylor. Any trace of fixtures and fittings had been removed. The only shapes to be found belonged to the shadows. I left the room and followed the L-shaped hall that took me past what might have once been a kitchen, and around to the front door.

The Yale lock was on a snib. I rotated the oval-shaped lock anticlockwise and the door assumed a gentle curve as it opened noiselessly. I walked out into the corridor and looked right and left—and saw a boy standing not far from me.

'Hullo,' I said. 'What's your name?'

He simply waved.

'Is there an adult around? Your guardian?'

He pointed up the way. The boy was as silent as the door I had just opened.

I said, 'Second floor?'

The finger remained pointing heavenward. I was careful to keep my distance. He was slim, but not gaunt. His hair dishevelled, but he wasn't filthy. *No mockit* as my old mum might have said. I noticed he wasn't wearing shoes.

'Third floor?' He began to rock from side to side, up on one foot then the other. Children were not my strong point, but I could tell he was agitated. 'Not third floor.' I paused and took a moment to reflect. There probably was no adult, there probably was no guardian. All I could be certain of was that there were thirty floors. 'Top floor?'

A smile on his face. So placated, the boy dropped his

hand to his side. I had a decision to make. I'd passed the point where I could be a one-woman army. I needed to phone this in.

As the phone rang, I motioned for the boy to stay put, not that he looked interested in going anywhere. A voice emerged from the other line. 'Hullo,' I said, 'Child services? Can you put me through to Kathy?'

I spoke to Kathy. Brought her up to speed regarding the child, not going as far as claiming he was abandoned, but he was alone in a condemned building which was scheduled for demolition. That was more than enough.

Quick, efficient, the call was over in the blink of an eye. I returned my attention to the boy. 'Do you know a way out of here?' I asked. (One I hoped didn't involve shards of glass sticking out of a window frame.)

Mercifully, the boy led me to another flat. A room cluttered with rubbish. A floor of newspaper and plastic, covering things lurking underneath that I'm sure were a lot worse. And I won't say what was on the walls, but it wasn't anything like Taylor Swift. It wasn't a remotely safe environment for a shoeless boy. I turned to him and lifted him up. The boy was as light as a feather.

I navigated carefully towards the window on a latch, which was showing signs of wear and tear but was functional.

I grabbed the latch, pushing open the window (thankfully still intact) as far as I could. I parked the boy on the ledge and then we waited.

Around about five minutes later, a uniformed officer appeared.

'It's okay,' I said, and resumed lifting the boy out of the window and over to the officer on the outside. It was effortless. There was no prospect of muscle fatigue in the arm that had held him. If I let him go, it wouldn't have surprised me if he floated all the way up to the sky. I was grateful for the officer's steady grip on the other side. It was a seamless handover. No drama. I was insanely grateful for the fact.

'You're getting a reputation, Ma'am,' she said, 'we'll be calling you Mother Theresa.'

'Fudging Mother Theresa,' I said. 'Look after him will you.' And then to the boy. 'I'll see you soon, I promise.' It was a promise I was determined to keep, at least right there and then.

The boy rewarded me with a big smile, a beaming one. Another precious moment. Again, it felt like I was making a difference. That I wasn't simply going through the motions. There was a live pulse in amongst the dead weight. There was an open window in front of me and I knew I'd reached the point, the absence of doubt, that I'd need to turn away. That I'd need to turn back.

'I need more time to check on something,' I said. 'I have reason to believe there are civilians in the building, possibly incapacitated.'

'Ma'am?'

I reflected on my last statement. I had no proof, not even a hunch in the making. 'I hope there are people in there incapacitated,' I said. 'Or have an equally valid reason why we have an abandoned child in an abandoned building.'

'Ma'am?'

'I'll be thirty minutes tops.' I checked the time on my phone. 'Can you phone it in? Let Baird Street know?'

'Ma'am.'

I took my leave of the officer and the boy. I felt my legs wobble, but there remained enough momentum residing in my joints to push myself on. It occurred to me then that I'd never asked the boy for his name. Then again, I think it suited me to think of him only as a nameless boy.

I resumed the trek through the ground floor. The corridors seemed more alive, there were more colours, not just ash grey. In sharp contrast, it was unnervingly quiet. There was no sign of life.

I was sure there were ghosts waiting to be found instead.

I came across a service delivery lift and decided nothing ventured nothing gained. I hit the call button. The arrow lit up, which heralded rumbling coming from above. The whole building was shaking. Maybe the upheaval was enough to bring the building down. Perhaps I might have saved the council a small fortune in explosives. But this was all flight of fancy. It was just a noisy lift, operational, but prone to groaning every inch of its descent. It took an age, but eventually the service delivery lift door swung open with a thunderous clatter. Of course, it would have to be that. I wasn't expecting a flourish.

I could see inside that there was ash and cinders on the floor, a crumpled curling black mass, evidence of a fire having been lit. There was some superficial damage, nothing structural, and it was far from spacious. There wasn't the capacity to deliver an adult elephant, for example. The one that insisted on following me around in rooms. And cars. Okay, bad example, but it didn't make the lift less operational. It came down to a leap of faith.

I was dogged by existentialist dread. Should I take the lift? If I get stuck somewhere, between floors, then so be it. I was surrendering myself to the uncertainty of fate. I just had to step forward and stand in the cinders and note that the lift only went up to the Fourteenth Floor. I saw it as a calculated risk rather than a gamble. There was a difference, I'm sure there was.

The lift trundled into life with me entombed inside. A little square window was my only gateway to the outside. I passed through a lattice of concrete beams and timber joists interspersed with one generic floor of apartments after another. Still, there was no sign of life. If there were any occupants in the Flats still, they weren't expecting a delivery.

I was alert, my brain was wired. Jangling. My thoughts roamed everywhere, there were no barriers. I thought about the boy. What kind of childhood had he—was he—having? Could he verbalise in a way that my non-maternal brain would understand? Would I ever be capable of talking on his level?

At his age, I'd had a happy home. No hang-ups. Dad worked nightshift as a shunter for the railways, coupling and uncoupling trains. I didn't understand all the ins and outs of what he actually did, but I knew the routine; he would leave for work when I was asleep and arrive back home in the morning when I was eating breakfast. He would bring home a selection of yesterday's newspapers, which people would leave on the train. I loved reading the news. I was fascinated with the idea of a much bigger world around me.

When I look back at that time, I attach so many feelings of security and certainty to Dad. He was always poised and measured in what he did. He wasn't erratic. He never made mad, sudden movements. His cuddles at Christmas and on birthdays; I remember how those arms could wrap around me three times over if he'd wanted. They made me feel safe and loved, like I was in a cocoon.

It was only later, when he was made redundant, that the mask began to slip. He'd pick up the odd job here and there, but nothing that was approaching permanent. He became fitful, never really at peace, and the creeping uncertainty had an effect on all of us. Dad was never the same after that, and neither were Mum and me.

My reverie was broken by the lift door, which emitted a fearful clunk before deciding to trundle open. This apart, I'd made it to the Fourteenth Floor without incident. It was a relief to get out of such a confined setting. I discounted searching for another lift. I decided I'd already rode my luck with this method of travel. What surprised me more was the conviction not to step back into the lift I'd just vacated and go straight down. I began to think of it as a kindred spirit. The service lift was a fish out of water, and so was I.

I was aware that if this was the movies, the audience would be screaming at me to go back. But this wasn't the movies. I was following a hunch, which in all probability I'd need to flesh out as a possible lead, when my superiors deemed to ask me about it. Ask me what possessed me.

The sign for the stairs pointed me to the far-end of the corridor. On the way, I encountered a flat without a door, nowhere to be seen, taken clean off its hinges. Still clinging to the idea I was on a recce, there was nothing stopping me from entering, not even a door. So, I took a look.

This wasn't a natural place for natural light, but I took big, confident strides anyway, sure of the ground beneath my feet. It was wooden flooring after all. It was almost like I was sleeping and I'd left my head at the doorway without a door. I came to with my foot dangling over a big fudging hole in the floor. At least three feet across, but if you'd put me on a lie detector test, I'd swear it wasn't there before. Until it was there, that is. Never in danger of losing my balance but in the grip of an ungainly pose, a little wobbly, before withdrawing my leg to surer ground. Surer in terms of the flooring creaking, bending a little. It was a case of creaking all round, coming to terms with the recklessness I'd shown moments before.

I took another step back and determined it safe enough to peer down. Looking back up at me was a middle-aged man dressed in what could pass for a welder's suit. He had his hands behind his back. We locked stares for a few moments before he took a few steps back himself, excising him from my line of sight.

I was taken aback by the speedy exit, which might explain why I hesitated in calling after him and asking something on the lines of whether he'd misplaced a child. Asking if he was keeping his nose as clean as his welder's outfit. It was nonsense. When did life get so ridiculous? I negotiated my own exit strategy, backtracking out of the room while part of me questioned, not for the first time, what I was doing here. What was the plan? No different from any other case: I was looking for answers. Maybe I would find some on the top floor.

I had the sense of undergoing a journey that wasn't ready to end, not right now. I took the stairs and started to climb. There were so many steps in front of me, they began to merge and dissolve into fuzziness.

It was a heart attack which took Dad from us. He was with us and then he was gone. A flick of a switch. A click of a finger. There was no time to even say goodbye. When Dad died, we tried to continue as normal, but what was normal? His imprint was already on us. There was a restlessness. I needed to watch what I said around Mum, even the most innocuous thing. I remember using the word 'tragic' when describing the Eurovision Song Contest on the telly. From Mum, this resulted in a flood of tears. For her, there was only one event that merited that word (and it didn't involve a soft rock ballad from Austria). And because my mum was crying, I'd be crying too. And I learned that there was power in words. There could be power in almost anything, whether you meant for it to be or not.

I ascended unimpeded a half dozen flights of stairs. It left me a little breathless, a little worried I was depriving my brain of oxygen. The tops of my legs were tired, aching for a change of pace.

They got one. From the landing of maybe the Twentieth Floor, I took pause. Mid-flight, just above me, some of the furniture and fittings missing from the flats on full display. A mishmash of chairs, tables, sofas, kettles, microwaves, and something which was, I don't know, shaped like a canoe. All brought together to form a barricade, or that's what it represented to me. It stretched from being pressed up against the wall on one side and the handrail on the other. There was little to suggest what was keeping it suspended or compact, a fixed point on the stairs. If I attempted to rearrange any of it, it seemed pretty clear that it wouldn't take much to bring the whole structure crashing around my ears.

Was that it, then? The end of the line? I was on a

stairwell one side of the building. For a tower this size there had to be another one situated the other side. If it was the end of the road, what did I have to lose by checking this out?

I wasn't sure what to expect on a floor this high up, more of the same probably. It wasn't quite like that.

The fire doors opened up to a row of giant dominoes either side. Every door was painted black. The walls were choked by graffiti. Graffiti slapped on graffiti, a nest of snakes stretching head to tail with no end. The snakes had fangs though. The phrases daubed on the wall I could make out were along the lines of: '*If you go out to the woods today*' and '*Vive la fucking revolution*' and (not my personal favourite) '*Fuck the homeless*'.

Words smeared on the actual doors were more succinct, ranging from '*No Entry*' in white paint on several, to a red cross painted on others, to '*Fuck off and die*' on another. And after that I stopped reading.

I put my head down, but I couldn't empty it. Thoughts were never far away. Thoughts that finally turned to him, the DI. We all have our demons, it came with the territory, but his were more obvious; more real. No greys with him, just black and white. Maybe, in this respect, he was a true trailblazer—that life should be that uncomplicated. You knew where everyone stood, took them on face value, no ambiguity. No need to look further than the end of your nose to know your true enemy.

My true enemy was the world. It had hurt me. I'd had cause to report the DI, just cause (or so I thought), and the three Wise Men called me to account. The system I had so loyally served turned on me and ripped me into pieces and reassembled me, so they could refashion me in a form they could tolerate and send me out again to do their work. But it was worse than that, because the version of me they'd created I now despised. I was one of the good guys, but apparently that wasn't good enough for them, so they sucked the life out of me.

Mum, you weren't there when I really needed you. In the end, you were a husk of a person. Ravaged by a disease that wasn't your fault, a by-product of living. I loved you with all my heart, an unconditional love, but even that wasn't enough. And then you were taken away from me, completely.

All I wanted was for no barricades to stand in front of me. I reached the end of the corridor and I looked up and I got my wish. As far as the eye could see, there were uninterrupted stairs. I took the stairs two, sometimes three, at a time. The echo of my feet on stone steps seemed to be simultaneously in front of and behind me. I felt stronger than I had felt for some time.

It was as if the real me was emerging after a long deep sleep, and the purpose of the climb was to expose this impostor after all this time. The one who had taken my place—who was walking in my shoes.

I had a renewed sense of purpose and it meant everything to me. I was aware of the sweat on my brow, the fact my face was flushed, the tightness in my lungs.

I was aware, but I ignored it all the same. The last few flights of stairs hardly registered at all.

And I knew I could turn things around. 'I'm not going to take this shite anymore,' I said for the benefit of the emptiness around me. It was my first swear word spoken in earnest in a year, and possibly a day (not that I was counting), and it only took thirty storeys to get there.

I had made the top floor. Not that I had any plans in place now I was here. I had an invisible rope stitched into me. I could feel the tug. Nothing to add, except keep on walking.

On the floor in front of me, there was what once must have been a door mat. A heavy-duty one; coir by the look of it. From my viewpoint the mat was glistening, soaked in a dark, heavy liquid. Some of the fluid had escaped into little pools which creeped beyond the rough surface. It could have been a welcome mat, but in its present condition it was impossible to tell.

The door, as way of extension to the mat, was ajar. From behind the door, I could hear the remnants of a conversation. Heavy, guttural, hushed, two similar voices from what I could ascertain. I couldn't make out any of the words. I tried to keep clear of the sodden mat, widening my stance, positioning myself to carefully push open the door. Even so, the going was soft and sticky underfoot. The door, however, showed no resistance.

From beyond, there was a deepening thud, a hollow

sound, followed by muffled whining, a long, restrained shriek.

I had no sooner caught my breath than I lost it again. The scene in front of me was grotesque. It was carnage. On one side of the room was a man in a pig mask, which was torn at the crown. I presume he was a man. He was standing, unsteadily, in front of a table which had hairpin legs. It didn't appear the sturdiest of structures, but then again neither did he. He was painfully thin. His left hand was tucked in between his right side and arm. On the table was a machete, the blade saturated in a puddle of blood, pink tubes forming an arch around it.

'No,' I said.

And there, sprawled out on the other side of the room, was the DI. A tattered facsimile of a man. His punctured body looked like it could float away on its own blood. Still, it didn't seem like he was too perturbed by the situation he found himself in. Momentarily, I was sure, I caught a look of animalistic defiance. A look I had seen at least one time before.

He smiled at me and for a second I really wanted to smile back.

'No.'

I clutched my phone in hand. This wasn't a recce, a flight of fancy, not anymore. I couldn't rely on the half hour being up, even if my thirty minutes was used up some time ago. I needed to call this in.

I still wasn't sure who I was looking for. I was looking for the Balaclava Man, be it Peter McGarvey (the name in the text) or whoever. I was looking for the DI. I was looking for a man in a mask.

I looked up from my phone. The man in the pig mask was standing four to five feet from me. He held up his fingerless left hand for me to see. The machete had done its work cutting off four fingers. Such was the ferocity and breadth of the stroke, it halved his thumb also. All the way down to the elbow, his arm glistened red. He held a firearm in his other hand.

'What do you see?' he said. His voice was a collection of sounds that somehow happened to form something meaningful.

Instinctively, I manoeuvred my frame, a half-defensive, half-offensive posture. He mirrored my actions, choosing, for whatever reason, not to revert to the gun. Not quite mirrored. His feet slipped on the greasy, bloody surface. His legs gave way underneath him. He fell forward, a graceful arc; only gravity, and whatever luck he was privy to, joining him on his way. He cracked his head on my knee.

It was difficult with the mask to tell what part of his head hit me. It didn't matter. It shouldn't have mattered.

My knee erupted in pain. It was no longer part of me, wanted to break out of me. It wanted to crawl out of my skin. It wanted to crawl out of my bone.

Down we both went; down on the hard wet floor.

I needed to get back on my feet. I needed to get up first. Scrambling on the floor, my body roiling the slick surface, creating a human-sized suction pad. I had no choice but to slow down, reach out with both hands. Turn and keep turning, slipping, sliding, until I was up on all fours. From my new vantage point, I didn't want to look; I would rather turn away. I just needed a moment to reconfigure things in my mind.

I looked across and saw that the man in the latex mask was laid out on his side. His expression was impenetrable to me, and all the more vivid because of this. The gun was now on the floor, closer to his feet than his hand. I saw that he wasn't moving.

I pushed up. I was in a crouched position. I pressed down on my tongue with my top molars as my busted knee let me know its displeasure. I needed to start climbing again. Up and up.

I found the DI filling my vision once more. I saw the curling lip, which could only now be meant for me. It was enough to confirm what I thought I'd seen before, and it was only there for a moment, half a moment, before giving way to the pallid features of man bled half to death.

Maybe even more than half.

*** *

I had no idea how she'd found me. Good old DS Spenc...

...Spence...

...Spencer...

I was flitting in and out of consciousness, but was determined even so, that I would not ask her how she found me. I wouldn't form the words. I would keep it a mystery. That, or wait until she told me of her own voliti...

...volitio...

...volition...

I had got so good at dying, I was afraid it had become something of a habit.

And now I had to sit it out and wait for the cavalry to arrive and tend to my never-ending wound. Which was fine really, sitting it out was the only option, at present, open to me.

She checked Peter McGarvey's body for a pulse, a sign of life. She struggled to find one. It was probable that the second knock of the head, down on the concrete floor, did more damage, but I liked to think it was DS Spencer's knee which served the same purpose for the second Peter as a Bar-L shower wall had done for the first.

And on the subject of knees used as a blunt instrument, I should know because I had previous ... *He* had previous ... *I. He.* It was so hard to distinguish these things. There was so much blood. It collected at the soles of my feet. Whether it was his blood or mine, it didn't seem that important. I was losing my grip.

DS Spencer had entered the bathroom to look for a towel but had decided against the one she found, which was encrusted in filth. She couldn't have it in the same room as, never mind anywhere near, an open wound. Instead, she produced a toilet roll which she unspooled round and round, handing me a cat's cradle of jumbled paper. Somehow, my bleached trembling hands were able to take the sprawl from her. She guided said hands, urging me to hold and press the tissue hotchpotch against my punctured chest. I could have sworn there was handwriting on the toilet paper.

She did all this through gritted teeth, she could hardly stand. She took off her jacket and turned it inside out. She directed it so it followed the same path as the sprawl. I momentarily had it within me to look down and saw that the toilet paper was already reduced to a pulpy crimson mess, thankfully obscured a second later by the blue lining of her jacket.

Light blue. It made me think of the sky, of the chirping birds.

The fucking chirping birds.

I was suddenly aware of DS Spencer looking around the room, perhaps too frantically, disproportionately so, when compared to the horrors that had gone on just before. It was part of some kind of coping mechanism, possibly, the need to ask innocuous questions suddenly taking hold of her like a puppeteer might grip a Marionette's strings.

'DI...' I heard her say. I'd always been two letters to her—'D' and 'I'. She'd be as well adding an 'E' at the end for good measure. 'Your walking stick,' she said. 'No stick today?'

And then it came to me, through the fog and unformed shapes, the way she was hobbling from one point to another, she was probably asking for the stick for herself.

'I left it,' I said. Or I mouthed the words, unsure if

I was capable of actual speech anymore. 'Left it in the rub...'

'...rubbl...'

'...rubble of the 3 Pubs,' I think I might have said.

21.

Date No. 5

It was time for the Big Show, or the Conference of Parties, or COP for short. Leaders of the various countries which make up the planet flew into Glasgow to debate the dangers of burning fossil fuels, creating their own set of carbon footsteps along the way. Doing what leaders are good at, pointing fingers and spouting figures and putting the blame squarely on everyone but themselves. Demonstrators descended en masse, intent on venting their anger at the devastation wreaked on a cluttered planet, a rocky road of discarded Costa cups and empty Snickers wrappers left in their wake. Between this unstoppable force and immovable object stood the thin blue line.

Overheated humans, overheated planet.

Amid all the turmoil and recriminations, amid the violence both naked and implied, pushing back and buffeted in return, made to feel like a fishing boat at the mercy of rough seas, we kept the peace. For the most part we tried our best, and could at least seek solace in the fact that we were due a little overtime.

I didn't play favourites. I'd learned this so many times, and always the hard way. But was it too much to expect a little hope or a little cheer? Why did I take this job, this vocation, this career in the first place? Give us a little fudging hope.

There were no good cops here, or bad ones. We'd moved past all this. The stakes were so much higher. If this world was going to end, the least we could do was ensure it did so in an orderly fashion.

***

Peter McGarvey was dead. Almost. As good as. He was in a coma, the type doctors say that you don't recover from. No next of kin had come forward. In this respect, a room full of indecipherable notes left behind in a derelict flat was no help at all. It was just a matter of time before the decision was made to withdraw life support. I never got to know that much about him, but I'd found him anyway. I wasn't the first to find him, but I didn't have to understand why this was the case for him to die. I just had to be me, that's all.

My knee as a murder weapon; *he* had done as much for me. Not that McGarvey's inevitable passing would classify as murder in any legal or, to be accurate, true sense. I could hardly walk for several days afterwards. My knee was doing its best Mount Etna imitation.

And then I woke one morning, body rattling with anti-inflammatories, and I was back to normal. No swelling, no pain. Ligaments can be like that sometimes. Still, a minor miracle to call my own.

I declared myself fit for duty the next day. Me and the ghosts that follow me around. Throughout it all, I'd tried to be true to myself. And it was all a lie. A big fudging lie. Even from this far down below, you can still smell the shite.

***

There was still an agreement to be honoured. An arrangement. It was viewed by the other party as a bargaining chip. 'You must really want rid of those pants,' he'd said.

And I couldn't put up an argument against it. All said and done though, it wasn't something I wasn't looking forward to. He had a nice smile, a little lopsided, but it lent him character. It gave him transparency. He wasn't a liar, or at the very least should the occasion demand it, my instincts said, I could trust him enough to be straight with me. I was determined, should it come down to it, to be the same with him.

I'd had a couple of days off. My first block of time off for months. Since the advent of my Mount Etna knee, in fact. It was a bright, light evening and the sun dazzled in the sky. It looked like it had always been there, never obscured by cloud, or night even, making everything feel fresh and clean. The streets of Glasgow had never looked better. We met up at a corner pub in Merchant City. He was already sitting at a table when I got there. I still didn't know his first name.

'Agent Beale,' I said.

'Ma'am,' he said, lifting his head up from his phone.

I liked the fact we weren't on first name terms. Not yet at any rate.

'What are you watching?' I said.

'*The Bridge.*'

'Original or US remake?'

'The original,' he said, 'although I was thinking of learning Swedish to get away from having to read those tiny subtitles on my phone. Only to realise I'd need to learn Danish too.'

'How can you stand the crime? The drama?'

'Remember, I'm not a real policeman,' he said, 'I work in incinerators.' He was so impossibly earnest. 'I have to take any drama I can get.'

'Join the queue,' I said.

***

I would think often about the baby I rescued from Cathcart Road, but I followed up on the shoeless boy from The Flats. I had promised I would. More a promise to me than a promise to him.

Social services hadn't gotten much out of the boy. His name was Mark.

Mark was in emergency foster care. I was given the address, but I wasn't sure what to do, so I drove up and settled for parking on the street outside the house unannounced. I waited five, ten minutes, but it wasn't long before Mark turned up, holding hands with an adult female. They moved slowly together, carefully. The boy was smiling; he looked so different, and this took me by surprise. He was wearing shoes.

I stayed in the car. Mark moved his head, looked back. Maybe he looked in my direction, the most fleeting of glances towards me. Maybe, he saw me just for a second. If he had, I'd decided that would be enough.

I started the car. Although it was no longer giving me bother, I was still conscious of my knee. I worried it might start to ache again. It was something daft like that. I drove off.

***

I was climbing stairs. Again. The back of my legs groaned with 100% muscle memory. If they ever chose to make it an Olympic sport or an event at the Commonwealth Games, I'd be up there on the podium winning a medal for Scotland. This time I was only headed for the Fourth Floor, which normally passed for a warm up.

I wasn't feeling like a winner, though. Nothing was resolved. Constantly on the move and I couldn't stop to think. I couldn't trust my thoughts. In the Flats—the very top flat—I saw a man get away with it all over again.

Last night's date with Agent Beale was pleasant enough. It was more than pleasant. I don't even know why I'd use the word *pleasant*; I can be an arse sometimes. At the end of the night, he went to kiss me. I think he was aiming for my cheek, but I turned my head suddenly so he ended up planting one right on the kisser. It was only sort of half intentional on my part, but I wasn't displeased with the final result. But it wasn't right, he knew it wasn't right, I knew it wasn't right.

'I like you,' I said. 'I really like you, and just now that's a problem.'

It was a problem because I couldn't be myself, and I hadn't been myself for a long time. There had been the occasional high, the tiny victories as I liked to call them, but destined to be short-lived, and the lows that would inevitably follow threatened to knock the stuffing out of me. I worry that a part of me might be lost forever. And in its place, there's this husk, this thing. Just going through the motions, however efficiently I did so. A robot. A lifeless thing. Going to whatever lengths not to feel anything. Halfway through a book, when you get to the really interesting bit, only to turn the page and see nothing at all. A blank page. Not even an apology.

I saw the DI approach Anthony Dorrans, barely breathing, a knife buried in his chest. I saw the DI lean down and grip the handle of the knife and twist. I saw Anthony Dorrans take his last breath, and I saw his head fall to the side. I'd told the three Wise Men this. I filled in a report and was banished as a result. I can't stop going back to this, because none of it is resolved.

And then over a year later, I saw that expression again.

'*What do you see?*' I saw how his mouth twisted. No different to the twist of a knife. His voice was so low, impossible to hear. He'd said something to compel Peter McGarvey to take a machete to half his hand. I did not hear the words, but I know he said it. I saw it in his eyes. His soulless eyes.

It didn't lead him to me. It didn't lead directly to his death.

He didn't set me up. Was bleeding half to death himself any kind of excuse?

'*What do you see?*'

I know the world wasn't expected to mourn the passing of either Dorrans or McGarvey. Especially the latter with the things he did, but where was the justice? Me and the DI, and so many others beside, we'd sworn to uphold it. Justice applied to us as much as to everyone else. To do the right thing. Is it such an insane concept to cling to, even now in a modern age where the gods of cynicism and hate sway over all others? Am I the only one who still thinks like that? Am I the odd *man* out here?

'What do I see?'

What was I to do? He was on an operating table in the Queen Elizabeth fighting for his life, a bullet wound to the chest. He'd lost so much blood. More blood that any one person ever had the right to have. If he died, he'd be a martyr. Even more of a hero than ever, if such a thing were possible. He'd never face due process. He'd get away with it. He wouldn't need to live with it.

But I would.

I was put on compassionate leave last year. Bundled in with that was the option of speaking with a counsellor. The offer was repeated six months later when my mum died. Both times, I have to confess, I wasn't interested, but recently my resistance to the idea had lessened to the point I enquired if the offer had an expiry date. Apparently, I was informed, it did not.

I was in a rut and I needed to do something to get out of it. I couldn't make inroads in any kind of private life until I came to terms with my professional one, the latter having already consumed so much of the former. I was open to anything, and if talking to a professional might help, then I was up for it. I was born again. I surprised myself just how up for it I was.

I already had someone in mind. So, I climbed the stairs of a psychiatrist's practice on West George Street, which went by the name of *Cuthbert, Preston and Associates*.

When I reached the office on the Fourth Floor, she was already there in the lobby ready to meet me. For a moment I panicked and thought I must be late for my first appointment. But the clock on the wall told me I was five minutes early. I was grateful for this, such is my need for any reassurance going.

First impression was that she was an impressive person.

She exuded self-confidence. She looked like she belonged in her current setting; that it was an extension of her. If I was to spill my guts to her, ideally, I wanted to like her from the off and in this respect every little thing helped.

She held a notebook down at her side. She looked like one half of—what were they called again? I'd watched an old episode of them recently on iPlayer—they were pretty funny I think, from what I could remember—*French and Saunders*.

'Dr Preston?' I said, the words taking the form of half a greeting, half a query. Although, who else could it have been, really?

'Detective Sergeant,' she said. She placed the notebook down carefully on the reception desk next to her. 'We won't be needing this, not on our first session.'

'Call me Dawn,' she said.

***

Searing pain. Unbearable pain. The bullet tore a chunk out of me and it opened the floodgates. I left it all, and much more besides, back in the Flats.

And I was back in my home from home—back in a hospital bed. This time I was in a recovery room, hooked up to a ventilator, my best friends a saline drip and a bag of blood. There were so many tubes attached to me, I was Gulliver tied up by the tiny people of Lilliput.

Everything went dark. The walls, if indeed they

were walls, were dappled by concave shadows. A familiar shape announced itself with a clink of a glass. An emerging voice.

'You've come BACK then?'

The voice belonged to a malignant presence, painfully thin, next to no eyebrows. Flaccid eyelids. But any sense of menace was seriously undermined by the ridiculousness of the question. A facile and infantile question, which I had no intention of dignifying with a response. How could I possibly have come back when I'd never been away? He would need to do better than that.

Undeterred, blinkered, he went on. 'We are both FOOT soldiers, you and me. We both have our ROLES to play. The right side of the law, the WRONG side. It's like a DANCE, we give you a bloody nose, you give us a bloody nose. We both need the chaos in order to FEED from it—and that's where fuckers like you come in. I had my ORDERS. They came FROM up top, and you don't have to be a detective to know this could only come from Roy Lichtenstein, the only fucker I could ever answer to. He has PLANS for you. Not the snotty-nosed, by the book, meticulous PRICK you've been. He wants the BIG Man, the berserker, the unpredictable you. The lunatic BOBBY on the beat. The BITE-YOUR-EAR-OFF-AS-SOON-AS-LOOK-AT-YOU you.'

He held out a glass, brimming with malt whisky. Bruichladdich. I didn't know what he was going to say next, but I knew what type of whisky it was.

'My job was to drag YOU back out of hiding' he said. 'I'm a GOOD soldier, a trusted lieutenant to the death. FUCKING literally! I'm not the ONE giving out orders here. Big Roy WANTS the Big Man and Big Roy gets what he wants.'

There was no room for water in that glass, or ice, for anything less than 100 Proof.

'You KILLED me,' he said. 'HE killed me. Fell on me from a great fucking HEIGHT, and then you decided to take him away, exile him, hidden from sight. You had NO right. You're a fucking ERRAND boy.'

And I realised it wasn't Coleman in the shadows. I thought I was fooling everyone, but the truth was that I was fooling myself. I *was* the errand boy, and this had all been a fool's errand.

It was me in the shadows. And I was thinking it wouldn't hurt to reach out and take the glass. Maybe just take a sip. In spite of myself. In spite of the man standing in front of me. In spite of the whole miserable, malfunctioning situation I'd found myself in. And I was resigned to the fact that I couldn't stop a shit-eating grin from devouring my face even if I tried.

'Scumbag,' I said. My voice was deep.

'Fuckwit,' I said. My voice sounded like I'd been gargling with gravel. 'What kind of plans?'

...

Relentless pain. The crashing of waves against a

crumbling seafront. Pain that would not be ignored or was happy to play second fiddle. In response to this, life had taken a certain form, manifested in my mind, if only to emphasise the sensation of it pulling away from me. Elasticated life. Life as a rubber band.

Even when fighting for my life, I could still find time to reflect. A product of a ruthlessly efficient mind.

Three strikes and you're out.

Three strikes. Three times I'd needed to bring *him* back to save the day; at the Bar-L, the 3 Pubs, and finally, on the Thirtieth Floor of Victoria Flats. It was only the essence, a hint, a flavour of him. But who was I kidding, least of all myself? Because it was more than enough, it was him.

Him, him, him.

That was all it took for something fundamental to shift. Which meant I had already lost. Which meant that someone had to die today. After all the pain and suffering and interminable inner turmoil, it was only right. It had to be this way. It was only good and proper.

...

...

...

I had no idea what restarted first. It was a case of take your pick.

It could have been the searing pain in my finger, or what I kept calling a finger. It was either that or the breathing, the frantic intermittent breathing, greedily feeding off the ventilator.

I was dead back there for a few seconds. *As deid as a lamppost. Pan breid.*

But I was back now, energised, a glorious mix of enzymes, sugars, DNA and proteins. Enthusiastic recipient of a new lease of life.

I sat up, ripping off wires and tubes. Snapping them, just like the protagonist breaking free of his restraints in *Gulliver's Travels*.

I was aware of doctors and nurses scampering and buzzing around me, frantically looking for discarded robes, habits, and rosary beads.

'You're back,' one of them said.

I was back all right. Not just an essence or a phantom or a hazy reminder of a man that once was. This was an out-and-out, larger than life, lock-up-your-uncles-and-aunties, scrotum-kicking change. A bilious alteration. A demented makeover. I tore the oxygen mask from me. I'd had my fill of ventilated air. I flexed my neck, one side then the other, discharging a series of almighty cracks in the process. My eyes were bloodshot, which was impressive considering I had so little of the red stuff to spare. My hair was a mess, my chest was on fire. I felt the bulk of my reborn, engorged body bristle against my hospital gown.

I was the fucking cat's pyjamas.

I had found my voice, my true voice. They knew it, I knew it, and that's how it was going to stay. I clicked the fingers on my right hand and everyone, doctors and nurses, stopped in their tracks.

I said, 'Any of you fuckers miss me?'

Not that it mattered what anyone had to say in return.

Editor: Kirsten Murray
Proof: Elinor Winter
Production: Jim Campbell
Cover by Alex Ronald

Thanks to: Michael Clifford, Jim Cairney,
Liz Small, Ann Landmann, Stephen Slevin,
the Soccer Maws, John Fowlie, the Rennies,
Drew Gillespie, David Braysher, Ed Murphy,
Eli, Alex, Kirsten and (the other) Jim C

Website: jimalexanderwriting.com
Twitter: twitter.com/JimPlanetjimbot
Facebook: facebook.com/groups/planetjimbot

Contact Kirsten Murray at hello@kirstenmurray.co.uk

GoodCopBadCop and the Light (paperback and digital)
by Jim Alexander available from Amazon, Barnes and
Noble, Kobo, Etsy, and lots of other places, including
our...

Online shop:
www.etsy.com/uk/shop/PlanetJimbot

Other books by the writer of *Good Cop*

GoodCopBadCop

A modern crime take on Jekyll and Hyde where both *good cop* and *bad cop* are the same person. This is not a story about a good man turned bad, or a bad man turned good. Both good and bad arrived at the same time. We delve deep into the psychological trappings, black humour and surrealist overtones as we really get into the gut(s) and mind(s) of Detective Inspector Fisher.

the Light

On a daily basis, people are required to take the Light; a device that ascertains whether this will be their last day on Earth. The story alternates between showcasing and building up this new world and telling the story of an ordinary person having to cope in extraordinary circumstances. We will see through his eyes a world so achingly similar to our own, but different in one shattering, all-pervasive way. When approaching death, whether it's dying in your sleep or experiencing your whole life flashing in front of your eyes, in the end it is no longer a case of floating towards the light; the Light wants to find you first.

Case File

GoodCopBadCop started life as a comic strip, then as a Graphic Novel (published by Rough Cut). It was in the latter that DI Fisher made his debut in prose form in the shape of several Case Files. The Case Files were short and to the point, two things you wouldn't necessarily say about me if you met me in real life! I thought it might be fun to include one here. The eagle-eyed of you will recognise what follows as an early version of a scene, seen initially from the viewpoint of Good Cop, then Bad Cop, that made its way into the novel GoodCopBadCop—Jim Alexander

On the morning of my last day Clydebank and I were joined by Officer Jock O'Ready and his horse Tamson and Officer Bruce Kent and his horse Winchester. We were policing an anti-imperialism demonstration held in Govanhill. It was organised by the Proper Socialist Party with 43 demonstrators in attendance. Everything was pretty quiet, so Jock and Bruce had ridden off in search of a coffee. Leaving trusty steed and I to watch over people content to wave red flags and denounce Archdukes everywhere.

I heard a chomping sound. I looked down and saw some middle-aged ne'er-do-well feeding Clydebank half a sausage roll.

'What do you think you're doing?' I said.

'Giving the horsy a wee clap,' he said.

'What are you feeding him?'

Ne'er-do-well looked up at me as if I'd said something mad like there was life in Venus or at a stretch Pollokshields. Clydebank showed off his Royal Family teeth as the man waved the other half of the sausage roll in front of them.

'Please stop feeding the horse,' I said. 'It's not good for him.' This was true; a sausage roll or equivalent savoury foodstuff could give the beast potentially fatal colic. And in any case horses have strict vegetarian beliefs.

Blissfully ignoring me, he continued to feed the horse. So I got down from the saddle and put handcuffs on him. The action did not go unnoticed by the other 42 members of the demonstration.

'Arrested for giving a horse a clap,' a voice shouted out from the gallery.

The crowd's shackles were up. It edged closer, circling ne'er-do-well, me and horse. 'Fucking imperialist,' one of them said. Another voice, 'fascist'. 'Belgian,' went another one.

All the while Clydebank's eyes were bulging and the eruptions from his tummy were something fierce.

This was my last day before starting in plainclothes and I had visions of my horse keeling over. Death by sausage roll. This was not good.

Something clicked inside me. 'Shut up you!' I scream into the ne'er-do-well's ear. My attention turned to the baying crowd. 'The rest of you, you're all under arrest.'

At this point my fellow officers Jock and Bruce returned on horseback, watery cappuccinos in hand.

'You've arrested the whole demonstration?' Jock said. 'Who the fuck do you think you are? Judge Dredd?'

How else 12 years ago in Govanhill on my jack jones could I keep 42 demonstrators and one numpty at bay? By being polite to them and minding my Ps and Qs? I don't fucking think so! It was through the sheer strength of personality of being a nutcase. They knew at any moment I could pounce on any one of them and rip their fucking tongue out! That's the way to pacify the hoi polloi.

At the point officers Tamson and Kent on horseback returned to the scene, probably glad of the distraction from their pish-poor cappuccinos, I left my horse Clydebank with them and started frogmarching my prisoner to a police van parked the other end of the street. On route we passed a Greggs the bakers and I popped in and bought five piping hot Bridies.

Bridies are Scotland's equivalent to pasties. They originated in Forfar. You know the classic score line

East Fife 4 Forfar 5? It's that Forfar! It consists of minced steak, butter, onions and seasoned beef suet encased in flaky pastry. It forms a kind of rectangular shape, so maybe not the best of designs for eating, but comfort was the last thing I had in mind. I pushed the ne'er-do-well into a back alley and force fed him all 5 of the fuckers.

'How the fuck do you like it?' His hands were spinning but he couldn't answer gagging on minced steak stramash with add-ons. And they were hot – roasting – and I could smell his burning lips. At the end of it the ne'er-do-well was down on his knees, puking molten chunks and sobbing uncontrollably. I thought about going back to buy more Bridies, but decided he wasn't worth it. (They were 39 pence a pop.) Instead we continued on our way and I threw him in the back of the van and booked him. His name I'm not shitting you was Michael Jackson.

And that more or less concluded my last day with the mounted police. I just had time to pop into the horse equine unit at Blairfield Farm to say one last cheerio to my old pal and horse Clydebank. On arrival I was struck by the piercing tranquillity of the farm itself. You could hear something the size of a pin drop. It was enough to bring on a nose bleed.

I found Clydebank in his stable none the worse after the day's culinary adventure. A magnificent beast, still in his prime, still so much to give. We'd had two years together in service of Her Majesty policing demos, patrolling the city centre, and seeing grannies across the road. We'd officiated over a few Old Firm games in our time, being called an orange bastard by one side and a fenian bastard by the other; none of them bothering to enquire into our actual atheist leanings. Yeh we'd been through a lot.

My back hunched. My eyes settled on his majestic mane. I longed to kiss his throat. I longed to bite and tear a chunk out of it. But back then it was still early days and Dick Van Dyke was back on the case, keeping me – the other me – in check.

'First day as plainclothes tomorrow,' I thought out loud. Clydebank looked at me with an expression that said go boil your head. But that might have been the sausage roll talking. I straightened my back and puffed out my chest and blew the beast one last kiss goodbye.